Irving Robbins Middle School
Library
20 Wolf Pit Road
Farmington, CT 06032

CHRONICLES
OF THE
RED KING
The Stones of Ravenglass

ALSO BY JENNY NIMMO:

CHRONICLES OF THE RED KING

The Secret Kingdom

CHILDREN OF THE RED KING

Midnight for Charlie Bone

Charlie Bone and the Time Twister

Charlie Bone and the Invisible Boy

Charlie Bone and the Castle of Mirrors

Charlie Bone and the Hidden King

Charlie Bone and the Beast

Charlie Bone and the Shadow

Charlie Bone and the Red Knight

THE MAGICIAN TRILOGY

The Snow Spider

Emlyn's Moon

The Chestnut Soldier

Griffin's Castle

The Dragon's Child

Copyright © 2012 by Jenny Nimmo

All rights reserved. Published by Scholastic Press, an imprint of Scholastic Inc.,
Publishers since 1920. SCHOLASTIC, SCHOLASTIC PRESS, and associated logos are
trademarks and/or registered trademarks of Scholastic Inc.

No part of this publication may be reproduced, stored in a retrieval system, or transmitted in any form
or by any means, electronic, mechanical, photocopying, recording, or otherwise, without written
permission of the publisher. For information regarding permission, write to Scholastic Inc.,
Attention: Permissions Department, 557 Broadway, New York, NY 10012.

Library of Congress Cataloging-in-Publication Data

Nimmo, Jenny.
  The stones of Ravenglass / Jenny Nimmo. — 1st ed.
    p. cm. — (Chronicles of the red king ; bk. 2)
  Summary: Timoken has been living in apparent safety at Castle Melyntha with his sister, Zobayda, but
when he is betrayed and attacked, he is forced to flee into the forest with his magic camel and the wizard
Eri, leaving his sister behind.
  ISBN 978-0-439-84674-5 (jacketed hardcover) 1. Magic — Juvenile fiction. 2. Camels — Juvenile
fiction. 3. Brothers and sisters — Juvenile fiction. 4. Voyages and travels—Juvenile fiction. [1. Magic —
Fiction. 2. Camels — Fiction. 3. Brothers and sisters — Fiction. 4. Voyages and travels — Fiction.]
  I. Title. II. Series: Nimmo, Jenny. Chronicles of the Red King ; bk. 2.
  PZ7.N5897Sto 2012
  813.54 — dc23
                                    2012003034

10 9 8 7 6 5 4 3 2 1   12 13 14 15 16

Printed in the U.S.A. 23

First edition, June 2012

Book design by Elizabeth B. Parisi and Kristina Iulo

CHRONICLES
OF THE
RED KING
The Stones of Ravenglass

JENNY NIMMO

SCHOLASTIC PRESS / NEW YORK

For Eve

CONTENTS

PROLOGUE

Timoken, the African, has been in Britain for a year now. He had arrived with his sister, Zobayda, and five children whom he'd met in France: Berenice, from the Spanish kingdom of Castile, and Mabon, Edern, Gereint, and Peredur from Britain. Timoken, a magician, had saved them from a band of kidnappers.

The boys had persuaded Timoken to travel back to Britain with them, and Berenice, the adventurer, had joined them. On their long, dangerous journey the travelers formed a bond of loyalty and friendship that each knew could never be broken. Timoken made enchanted swords for them, and shields that they decorated with their chosen symbols: a bear for Mabon, the oldest and strongest; an eagle for red-headed Edern, who wanted to fly; a fish for Gereint, whose clear voice was like a singing stream; and a wolf for Peredur, with his long, pointed teeth. Berenice loved to run and she chose a hare. Timoken's shield was emblazoned with a burning sun, a memory of Africa.

When their kingdom was invaded, Timoken and his sister wandered, homeless, through the world for more than two hundred years. The four Britons had been born in Castle Melyntha, and their prince made Timoken and his sister so heartily welcome that, for the first time since their wandering began, they felt they had found a home.

CHAPTER 1
The Arrow

In the deep, dark heart of the forest, Timoken was happy. He might have missed the heat and brilliance of his African homeland, but here, in Britain, there was magic in the autumn leaves spinning through narrow shafts of light.

A bell sounded in the distance and Timoken began to make his way back to Castle Melyntha. He was approaching the edge of the forest when something swept so close to his cheek, he felt it burn. Whirling around, he saw the arrow, its lethal tip embedded in an oak. Would there be another arrow? Did someone want him dead?

A minute later, he got his answer. A second arrow came hissing through the air. There was a moment when Timoken could have leaped aside and used a tree to shield himself, but the danger had fired his quick mind, and he knew it was time to test his skill. He noted the arrow's trajectory and held up his arm. He had an instant of doubt as the arrow came at his unsteady hand but, incredibly, it hovered, an inch from his palm, and when Timoken uttered the ancient words from his homeland, the arrow slid into the air, turned, and flew back to the archer who had launched it.

There was a groan of pain and a soft thud as a body dropped into the undergrowth.

Timoken waited. Was the archer alone, or were there others, even now, marking him out and raising their bows? He moved behind the oak and listened. But the forest was silent. There were no footfalls, no rustling grasses.

"Have I killed?" Timoken stared at his palm. He had never used his hands to do what he had just done. But perhaps his cloak had protected him. Timoken wore a cloak that he had brought with him from Africa. It was made from the web of the last moon spider the world would ever see. It had protected Timoken for more than two hundred years, though you would have found that difficult to believe, for the boy looked no older than twelve years.

It was time to find out who had tried to kill him. Bent double to avoid any more deadly weapons, Timoken sped through the forest. The arrow had come from the direction of the castle. The trees thinned out as he drew closer to the edge of the forest. He found the body in a clearing, the bow still clutched in a gloved hand. A rough leather helmet covered half the face, but there was something familiar about the square chin and line of whiskery hair above the wide mouth.

Kneeling beside the body, Timoken carefully pushed up the leather helmet. "Mabon?" Timoken couldn't believe his eyes. His friend's pale blue eyes were still open, and gazed up at the sky in shock.

"Mabon!" cried Timoken. "Tell me it wasn't you."

Mabon didn't reply. The arrowhead had pierced his chain-mail tunic, and blood trickled from his chest.

"Why?" Timoken stood up and looked back at the castle, just visible through the trees. "Who sent you?" He rubbed his head and felt the slim gold crown buried in his black curls. "Who wanted him dead?" he asked himself. "And how had they persuaded Mabon, surely against his will, to try to murder a friend?"

For a moment, Timoken was too bewildered to move. He had left the castle alone, to stroll in the forest he loved. The drawbridge was down and the great doors open to receive traders. He had intended to slip back before the doors were closed for the night, but now what should he do? He couldn't leave Mabon like this, out in the trees where wolves and wildcats would find him.

Perhaps he could carry the body back to the castle, thought Timoken, and blame his death on bandits that roamed the forest. No. That wouldn't do. Whoever had sent Mabon to kill him would guess the truth.

It was the feel of his own cloak, warm under his fingers, that brought Timoken to his senses.

"The cloak!" he exclaimed. Pulling it from his shoulders, he quickly laid the cloak over Mabon's body and, gazing into the pale blue eyes, began to murmur in his own secret language. But Mabon didn't move, didn't breath, and there was not a flicker of life in the shocked blue eyes.

It was too late for Timoken to run. He could hear the tramp of feet and the swish and rustle of men beating a path through the undergrowth. At that moment he could have escaped, for Timoken could fly, but his abilities were secret, and each of the five friends who knew he was a magician had kept their word and, so far, had never betrayed him.

Grabbing his cloak, Timoken pinned it back on his shoulders, just as four soldiers stepped out of the trees. One glance told them all they wanted to know. In a second, Timoken's arms were roughly clasped and, while two soldiers held him still, the others bent over Mabon's body. Timoken recognized them. Aelfric, a broad-shouldered bully who was missing half an ear, and Stenulf, an ugly fellow with a nose like a pincushion.

"Sir Osbern won't like this." The soldier holding Timoken's right arm almost yanked it out of its socket. "Mabon Ludd was the sharpest of all our young archers."

"I didn't kill him," Timoken protested. "I . . . I found him. It must have been bandits."

"With an arrow like that?" Aelfric growled. "Bandits don't have fine arrows. They use spears and axes."

"I don't have a bow." Timoken winced as the soldier on his left twisted his arm. It was all he could do not to cry out. "How could I have killed, without a bow for my arrow?"

"So where is it? Hidden back there?" Stenulf's gloved fist slammed into Timoken's shoulder.

The pain took his breath away. "I told you. I don't have a bow," he gasped.

"Come on, we're wasting our time out here." Aelfric pulled out the arrow and, with his thumb and forefinger, deftly closed Mabon's eyes. "Stenulf, help me with the body."

Stenulf lifted Mabon and threw him over Aelfric's wide shoulder. They strode away, while the other two soldiers dragged Timoken after them.

As they reached the drawbridge, Timoken looked up into the pale sky. The low sun had gathered strength and begun to gild the mist with droplets of gold. He thought of using the fire in his fingers to free himself, he thought of escaping up into the golden mist, he even thought of calling eagles to attack his captors, but he knew he could do none of these things, for where would he go without his friends?

They marched him over the drawbridge and across the great enclosure where men hammered and sawed, where pigs rooted in the churned earth and sheep bleated in their pens. There was such a clamor that Timoken couldn't hear Aelfric's shouted command, but a carpenter hastily moved a bench barring the soldiers' way. Several men stopped their work and stared up at the body hanging from Aelfric's shoulder. Sadly, it was a common sight. The forest was a dangerous place; bands of outlaws hid in the depths: men who had lost everything to the conquerors but refused to accept their laws.

Timoken heard a sudden, high-pitched call that carried above the din in the enclosure. Someone was shouting his name.

"What's going on?" Red-headed Edern jumped over a bale of straw and ran up to Timoken. "What's happened, Timoken? Where are they taking you?"

When Timoken opened his mouth to answer, one of the soldiers jabbed an elbow in his face.

"Clear off!" shouted Aelfric. "This has nothing to do with you."

The boy leaped in front of the group, his freckled face creased with concern. "It's got everything to do with me," he cried. "I'm Edern, son of Elvin the poet. You wait till the prince hears of this. The great wizard, Eri, is my uncle, and you don't want to cross him or . . . or . . ."

"Or what?" With a sweep of his great arm, Aelfric shoved Edern aside, but the boy jogged beside the soldiers as they continued to drag Timoken along.

"Hey! What's happening?" Another boy had pushed his way through the crowd and appeared, breathless, beside Edern. "What've you done, Timoken?"

"Peredur—" Timoken began, but afraid of losing his teeth this time, he said no more and mutely shook his head.

"This isn't right. We'll do something, Timoken. I promise." The boy grinned, revealing two extraordinarily long, pointed teeth. His wolfish appearance could be rather alarming and he often used this to his advantage, grinning at his adversaries instead of scowling.

"Save your smiles, Wolf-face," said Aelfric sourly. "Your friend won't get away with murder."

"Murder?" Edern had been staring at the body slung over Aelfric's shoulder. He couldn't see Mabon's face, but he recognized the gloved hands of the archer.

"Murder," said Stenulf, leaning toward the boys. "Your friend has murdered Mabon the archer."

"No," Timoken burst out. A soldier's fist smashed into his chin, but he continued through swollen lips, "It's not true."

"Take the prisoner to the tower," Aelfric commanded. He grunted heavily as he mounted the steep steps to the castle. "I'll carry our dead archer to his family."

Timoken's heart sank. Mabon's family had been good to him. What would they think of his treachery? "I didn't know," he muttered under his breath.

At that moment, the glove fell off Mabon's right hand. No one bothered to pick it up. If Timoken hadn't been staring miserably at Mabon's bare hand, he wouldn't have seen the sign: a slight movement of the fingers. And then it was gone, and the hand hung limply from the lifeless body.

His friends hung back as the soldiers pulled Timoken up the steps. He looked over his shoulder and shook his head. Edern and Peredur were staring at him in shock. Surely they didn't believe that he had harmed Mabon.

When they entered the castle courtyard, Aelfric turned through an arched door on his left. Stenulf carried on across the courtyard to the tall central tower. "Put him in the old man's cell," he ordered as he pulled open the heavy door into the tower.

A guard stepped in front of Stenulf, barring his way with a raised spear.

"It's me," Stenulf grunted. "Give them the key to the wizard's cell."

The wizard's cell? What was Edern's uncle doing here? Timoken wondered. The prince thought highly of Eri the wizard. Why had he been imprisoned?

The guard nodded and fumbled with a ring of keys hanging from his belt. Selecting a large, rusty-looking object, he handed it to one of the soldiers.

"Don't be long about it," called Stenulf as the prisoner was marched toward a shadowy set of steps.

Timoken had never got used to the damp, spiraling stairways of Castle Melyntha. A melancholy smell lingered on the steep, cold steps: a musty scent, putrid and dark. He had no choice but to follow the first soldier up the steps; the second man came close behind, continually prodding Timoken's legs to hurry him up.

They came, at last, to a long passage where a low door faced a narrow window slit. The lead soldier turned the key in the lock and the door creaked open. Timoken was pushed inside and the door clanged shut behind him. He stumbled over a pile of rags and fell onto the hard, planked floor. As he lay there, staring at the filthy straw beside him, the rags cursed softly.

Timoken sat up and looked into a pair of owl-like eyes, eyes the color of a storm cloud, mysterious and alarming. They belonged to the wizard, Eri.

"Sir, forgive me," Timoken murmured. "I didn't know . . . didn't think . . ."

The wizard raised his head and shook out his black and silver hair. He sat up and brushed dust and hayseeds from his shoulders, revealing the faded gold stars on his once splendid cloak.

Timoken tried not to stare at the great wizard. Men bowed their heads when Eri passed; they whispered behind their hands, "Watch out, here comes the wizard," afraid that he'd act against them and turn them into pigs, though he'd never done such a thing.

"You didn't think that a prince's favorite could end up as a pile of rags?" The wizard's chuckle was heaved out of his rattling chest with a stream of spittle. "Well, I knew you would soon be here, African. But what did you do to give them the excuse?"

"They say I killed an archer," said Timoken. "But not any archer. He was my friend, and yet he tried to kill me."

"And how did you kill him?" The wizard sat up.

Timoken hesitated. "With . . . with my hand, sir," he mumbled.

"Ah," said Eri, scratching his long nose.

"And yet I think he might still be alive," Timoken said, almost to himself.

"Either he is, or he isn't. Whichever the case, once in here, no one ever gets out."

"What is happening?" asked Timoken. "For you to be imprisoned the world must have turned upside down."

"Precisely." The wizard shuffled over to Timoken and sat beside him.

"Prince Griffith honored you," said Timoken, his glance traveling from the wizard's bruised cheek to his torn and bloodstained robes. "What did you do to anger him?"

"Not the prince, Timoken. Our prince has gone to war far over the ocean."

"And when he returns he will punish whoever did this to you," Timoken said hotly.

The wizard hung his head and muttered, "He will not return."

"How do you know?" Timoken was aghast. Prince Griffith had been good to him. When Timoken had arrived in Britain, the first African ever seen in that part of the country, the prince had welcomed him. He was allowed to dine and sleep with the boys of high rank, he took lessons with them, and wore the same clothes. Even Timoken's camel was treated with respect, and stabled close to the prince's favorite horse. Though the camel, being rather a proud animal, didn't consider this a favor.

"Tell me, I beg you." Timoken gently nudged the wizard, who appeared to have fallen asleep, for his eyes were closed and his chin rested on his chest.

Timoken raised his voice. "How do you know our prince will not return?"

Without opening his eyes, Eri replied, "I am something of a seer. That means that, on occasion, I can dream the future."

"And what did you dream?"

"Last night I saw our prince lying on the battlefield. 'I am dying, Eri,' he told me. 'Save yourself and the African. Leave the castle, for dark——' And then our fine young prince gave a moan and said no more."

"Dark?" Timoken didn't like the sound of that word. "Leave the castle, for dark . . . ?"

The wizard turned his stormy gaze on the boy. "He meant Osbern D'Ark, the castle steward. The prince has always known that Osbern hated me, and I suspect the same holds true for you. You are popular, Timoken, and something of a leader to the other boys. And then there is that hint of a golden crown in your black hair. Osbern is from a family of conquerors. He wants this castle and every man it holds. He will probably get his way."

"Why?"

"The prince was young and leaves no heir. He was rare among the British, in that he kept his castle, while all over the country, the conquerors turned families off their land. Young Griffith was safe because his mother was sister to a conqueror. But now . . ." Eri shook his head.

"I am afraid for all the prince's favorites, especially my brother, the poet, and my nephew, Edern."

"What will happen to them?"

Eri shrugged. "Osbern will find a way to get rid of them, no doubt. And your friend with the wolf's teeth will fare no better."

"Peredur? His father is the prince's most respected general," Timoken said.

"And if he has died at the prince's side, then it will be all up with his family."

"No." Timoken began to see the pattern now. He and his friends were slowly but surely being separated. Gereint had already been sent to a monastery. Mabon spent all his time with the archers, and Berenice was closeted with the women. "At least she is with my sister," Timoken muttered.

"Eh? What's that you say?" Eri said irritably. "My hearing's not so good."

"I was thinking of my sister," said Timoken. "If Osbern D'Ark means to keep me in this prison, what will become of her? It seems that you and I must escape from here, but I can't leave Zobayda behind."

"The conquerors have nothing to fear from women," Eri said. "They won't harm your sister."

"We have traveled so far, and for so long. I thought we had found a home at last."

"Hmm," grunted the wizard. "This was my home for sixty years; it's too late for me to find another."

"No, sir. Not true. I'll build a home for all of us." Timoken spoke without thinking. He immediately wondered how he could achieve such an impossible task. Getting to his feet, he stood on tiptoe and looked through the window. It was too narrow even for him to crawl through. He could see the autumn forest, stretching for miles beyond the castle fields. On the horizon, a ridge of blue hills could be seen, their shape softened by the mist. "There," he murmured. "That's where we'll go, Eri. Into the hills."

The old man said nothing, but when Timoken turned, he found the wizard's eyes on him. "Are you going to reveal yourself at last, African?" he said.

"Do you mean my . . . ?"

"Your gifts, yes. Your talents."

"Did my friend Edern tell you?"

"No." The wizard sounded almost angry. "My nephew kept your secret. I knew what you were the moment you arrived, and I've observed you flying through the night sky on your camel. You must think me a fool, boy. We are the same, you and I."

"Forgive me." Timoken looked away from the wizard's accusing gaze. "I have always respected you, sir. I didn't know that you had guessed."

"The time has come for you to use your magic, for it is beyond my skills." Eri stood and laid a hand on Timoken's shoulder. "Osbern would not have put us in this tower if he meant us to live. I daresay your friend, the archer, was threatened with death for himself and his family, if he did not kill you."

Timoken nodded. He had already worked this out for himself. He ran his hand over the stones and mortar around the window until they reached the thick oak frame. Slowly, his fingers felt their way through time. He touched the sapling that the oak had once been, and even the soft earth that had nurtured it. "I can do it," he said.

"Wait until nightfall," the wizard advised.

They sat together on the dusty floor, and Eri clasped his bony knees to his chest, muttering, "It is a long way to fall, boy, from this tower. I hope you hold some charm for avoiding broken bones."

"I will carry you," Timoken said simply.

A smile lit the wizard's face. "Ah." He patted Timoken's knee. "We are in with a chance, then."

CHAPTER 2
Escape

The meager light began to fade. Soon they were plunged into a gloom beyond darkness, with not even a candle for comfort. No one came to the door; not even a crust was thrown into the prisoners' cell.

"They mean to starve us," muttered Eri.

"When shall we go?" asked Timoken.

"It's early yet," said the wizard. "There will be feasting in the courtyard, animals to tend, and all the bedtime din."

Timoken slept a little, and then woke up. The wizard was snoring. The noise he made rebounded from the walls like dull thunder. Timoken stuffed straw into his ears, but it made little difference. At that moment, he would have exchanged any of his extraordinary gifts for a spell to stop snoring.

After a while, Timoken became aware that, behind the wizard's rumbling snore, there was a deep silence. He went to the tiny window. The stars were fading. It was time to go. He shook the wizard's arm and the old man mumbled and grunted. A second later he was up. Gripping Timoken's shoulder, he whispered, "Now or never, boy. Let's go."

Once again, Timoken ran his hand lightly across the stones beneath the window. He felt the hardened mud that bound the stones; he felt the hands of the workers who had toiled on building the tower; and he touched the river water that smoothed the stones and carried the mud. He thrust his hand into the mud and, using the secret language of his homeland, urged it to give way. A large stone fell at his feet, a piece of timber followed it, and then another; mortar trickled onto the floor and dust flew out into the night air.

"Well and truly done," remarked the wizard. "We're nearly there."

"Soon, soon!" Timoken's brown eyes were shining.

A minute later, there was a gap in the wall wide enough and low enough to step over.

"What do you suggest?" asked Eri.

"Put your arms around my neck and hold tight."

Timoken felt the wizard's strong, sinewy arms wind themselves over his shoulders and around his neck.

"Off we go, then," whispered Eri, and Timoken was surprised to feel the wizard's pointed boot give his calf a little kick.

"I am not a horse," Timoken complained as he stepped into the sky.

They floated gently down into the courtyard just as Timoken intended, but all the while, Eri kept hissing, "Over the wall, boy. Over the wall. We can't land here. The guards will catch us."

When he felt the earth under his feet, Timoken said, "I'm going for my camel."

"Your camel!" the wizard softly screeched. "Your camel." He leaped in front of Timoken. "There's no time for a camel. Come on, let's get over that wall."

"I need my camel," said Timoken.

"Need, need?" cried Eri. "I need my bag of tricks, but you don't see me running for them do you?"

Timoken moved around the wizard and raced toward the stables. The old man pursued him, cursing quietly. "You'll wake the horses, you'll wake the stableboys," he muttered.

"Leave the horses to me," whispered Timoken. "You can deal with the stableboys."

Before he lifted the latch on the stable door, Timoken began to murmur to the horses in the language that they knew. He told them to be silent, and to remain still. They were at rest now. The camel would be leaving, he told them, but they wouldn't be needed until first light. Even as he said this, Timoken realized that dawn was almost upon them. The stars were fading fast.

As he made his way past the horses standing quietly in their stalls, a boy suddenly stood up, swinging a lantern in Timoken's face. "Thief!" he yelled. "You shall not steal our horses."

"Hush, boy," said the wizard, striding into the lamplight. "You know me. I'm no thief. Your name is Eadric, I believe."

Recognizing the wizard, the boy said, "I know you, sir, but what is the African doing here?"

"He has come to see his camel," Eri said mildly. "The prince allows this."

Eadric relaxed a little. "We've been commanded to take our orders from Sir Osbern now." He sounded apologetic. "And we have been told that . . . that . . ."

"Speak up, boy," the wizard said impatiently.

Timoken noticed that the other stableboys had woken up.

They approached from both ends of the stable, nervous yet curious to know what was going on.

"Speak, Eadric!" ordered the wizard.

The boy looked down at his feet and mumbled, "We've been told that you are a traitor, sir."

"Ha!" The wizard shook his head and laughed softly. "And who told you that?" he asked, his laughter subsiding.

"Stenulf Pocknose," whispered one of the other boys.

"Oh, him!" The wizard shook his head. "The fool. Now, boys. I'm sure you want to earn some silver."

The boys stared at Eri, their eyes dancing in the lamplight. Timoken wondered where all this was leading. He had hoped that Eri would have come up with a small spell to send the boys to sleep.

The wizard produced a fistful of silver coins from the folds of his torn cloak. He began to toss them in the air with one hand, catching them in the other. Some slipped through his fingers, spun toward the ground, and then, of their own accord, flew up into the rafters. The boys watched, speechless. They put out their hands, but the silver discs whirled past them and flew to the end of the stable. They chased after the silver, giggling with excitement. Eadric hung his lantern on a post and followed them.

The sound of their soft laughter would normally have agitated the younger, friskier horses, but they remained calm, still held by Timoken's quiet command.

Timoken took the lantern and went in search of his camel. He wasn't in his usual stall. He'd been moved to the far end of the stable, a damp, dark place without straw or water. The camel was crouching, his head lowered forlornly; his eyes were closed, but he wasn't asleep.

"Gabar!" Timoken whispered in the camel's language.

The camel's thick lashes fluttered. He opened his eyes and said, "The prince's horse has gone."

"And so has the prince," Timoken told him.

Eri peered into the gloomy stall. "I suppose your camel can understand your grunting," he said.

"Naturally." Timoken grinned. "Otherwise I wouldn't grunt."

"It doesn't look eager for flight," the wizard remarked, giving the camel a quizzical look.

"His name is Gabar," said Timoken, "and I haven't asked him yet." Kneeling beside the camel, Timoken said, "We're going on a journey. Where's your saddle, Gabar?"

"They took it," said Gabar. "They took everything. Soldiers. They mean to eat me. I saw it in their faces." He stood up and shook himself. "You'll have to ride without a saddle."

Timoken stood and patted his neck. "No one's going to eat you, Gabar. But I'll have to find a seat for the wizard. He's coming with us."

Gabar eyed the wizard suspiciously; the wizard returned the look.

Timoken ran down the stable, searching for the camel saddle. He almost tripped over the stableboys lying in a heap, all fast asleep. Timoken smiled. So the wizard's silver coins were charms after all.

He found a sack and stuffed it with straw. Grabbing some of the leather harnesses, he ran back to the camel and, asking Gabar to kneel again, began to fix the sack on the camel's hump.

"A fine saddle." The wizard gave a reluctant chuckle.

Timoken adjusted a harness and fitted it over the camel's head.

In a resigned tone, the camel snorted, "And now I smell of horse."

Ignoring the camel, Timoken said, "After you, sir," and stood back to let the wizard mount. Eri rolled his eyes. "May the forest gods protect me," he murmured. "May the sun, moon, and stars take pity." Gingerly, he lifted his brown robe and sat astride the camel's hump.

"That's not the way, exactly," said Timoken, seating himself, cross-legged, in front of the wizard. "But it will do. You'll have to hold me fast while I take the reins. Gabar may not respond to your touch."

"Woooo-o-aaa!" exclaimed the wizard as Gabar lifted himself from his knees and made for the stable door.

There was a rosy glow in the eastern sky, and birdsong was beginning to rise from the forest. The watchmen by the great door didn't need a lantern to see the camel trotting out of the stable.

"Hold there!" a watchman called.

"Up, Gabar. Up!" cried Timoken.

The watchman blew his horn and, before the camel could get into his stride, two soldiers ran from a doorway in one of the corner towers.

"The prisoners are out!" yelled one of the soldiers.

A spear came through the air and Timoken cried, "Down, wizard!" as he ducked beneath the spear. The wizard's head bumped into his back and, hoping the old man hadn't been hit, he leaned forward and tugged the rough hair on Gabar's back.

"Up, up, up!" Timoken commanded. "Now!"

Gabar gave a loud snort and, not a moment too soon, Timoken felt the camel leave the ground.

For a moment the soldiers were too stunned to act, and then, snarling with fury, they flung their spears at the flying camel.

"Never thought I'd see the day," came the wizard's deep mutter.

When Timoken had first taught Gabar to fly, it had been an arduous and punishing experience for both of them. But now the camel could climb into the sky with little more than an encouraging tug. He had learned to ride the air with astonishing ease, and within seconds, Timoken and the wizard found themselves above the castle wall. Soon they were beyond the range of any spear and sailing above the forest.

"The blue hills, Gabar," said Timoken. "See? Beyond the trees!"

"Will there be sand?" asked Gabar. How he longed for sand. He hated damp earth, the tangle of weeds, cold mud, and stony streams. Every night he dreamed of the desert where he was born. Sometimes he carried his dreams into his waking hours, and pretended not to feel the freezing hand of the wind beating on his skin or the ice from the water trough rattling down his throat. He deafened himself to the sound of the rain and the grumbling of the horses in the stable.

"We will find sand," said Timoken, meaning to keep his promise. "Even if I have to make it."

"Make sand, Family? That would be a new thing." Family was the name the camel always used for the boy who rode him, for that's what Timoken had told him when they first flew together, more than two hundred years ago. They were "Family" to each other.

"I believe you two are hatching a plot," grumbled Eri. "There's too much grunting for my liking."

Timoken laughed. "We're talking about sand," he said.

The wizard sighed. "Of course, what else."

The hills that had looked so blue and gentle at a distance were beneath them now. They were not blue, nor softly rounded, but a long escarpment of pale gold rocks, dotted with bracken.

On the other side of the hills lay a great plain dissected by several rivers. And here there were small hamlets, and men working the tilled land; men, and women, too, who saw the camel pass right over them. Shading their eyes, the people stared and stared but couldn't believe what they saw: a flying beast with two riders, and a crimson cloak that swirled in the wind like a great banner.

Soon soldiers would come and ask about the camel, and people would try and describe what they saw.

The wizard guessed all this. Shouting into the wind, he cried, "Boy, we must find a safer place, a wilderness, many, many miles from here. Can your camel go much farther?"

"He can cross an ocean," Timoken replied.

"I should have guessed," said Eri.

They were still in the air when night clouds began to unfold across the sky. The clouds were the same color as the wizard's eyes: a dark and stormy gray.

"We should take a rest," Eri murmured, "and continue in the morning."

Looking down, Timoken saw a pale sweep of land, almost white in the dusk, and beside it, milky lines of foam rolling in from the sea.

"Sand!" Timoken cried. "Gabar, we've found sand."

The camel gave a bellow of delight and plunged toward the earth.

"Your camel acts fast," screeched the wizard, gulping air. "My eyes are rattling in my head."

They landed with a bump and a slight skid as Gabar's hooves dug into the soft sand. He crouched to let the riders off his back and the wizard tumbled sideways onto the sand, while Timoken slid down gracefully.

"Why here?" Eri complained. "There's nothing." He got to his feet and rubbed his bottom. "No wood to burn, no hares to catch. Nothing, nothing. We can't even drink the water, it will all be salt."

Timoken wanted to say, "My camel must sometimes be

rewarded." Instead, he nodded at the wooded hills beginning at the far end of the beach. "There are your trees, and your food, and probably a stream of clear water."

"Two miles distant at least," grumbled the wizard. "I have never seen such a long, miserable stretch of nothing."

"There are probably fish," Timoken remarked, looking at the sea. "And you don't have to walk. Gabar will be happy to carry us over the sand."

"I am numb," argued the wizard. "I cannot sit on a hump any longer."

Timoken couldn't hold back his laughter, and the old man, hearing his own grumbling voice, began to laugh, too.

Timoken ran to the sea, to bathe his hands and feet. The wizard ambled after him. The water had a refreshing, icy bite.

"Aaaah!" sighed Eri, as he splashed his dusty face. "I'd forgotten the sea's restorative power. I can go on now, boy. I can even sit on a hump."

The camel was galloping back and forth over the sand, bleating and burbling with delight. When Timoken called to him, he came and knelt obediently to let the riders mount. But he was impatient to be off again, and hardly had the wizard made himself comfortable than Gabar set out, galloping over the sand like a wild horse.

Eri groaned a little but didn't complain. They were heading for the woods where he could catch a hare or a pigeon, build a fire, and cook. He wondered what the boy could do. Almost anything, he supposed, with that hint of a crown in his thick hair, and with his flying camel, his animal talk, and the mysterious glitter in his red cloak.

The boy and the wizard looked at the woods, but they didn't see the eyes that watched them from the trees.

The watchers gazed at the galloping, humped beast, churning the sand with its great feet. They observed the dark-skinned boy and the tattered man coming closer and closer, and they wondered what they should do. Hide, or stand and fight?

CHAPTER 3
Tree Children

While Timoken gathered sticks to build a fire, the wizard went in search of food.

The camel rested. From the clearing that had been chosen for their night's rest, Gabar could see the wide stretch of sand, pale and gleaming in the dusk. He hadn't known such happiness for a long time, not since he and Timoken had arrived in this damp green land a year ago.

Eri appeared with a dead hare and a bag full of berries. "There are plenty of deer," he said, "but I wasn't in the mood for chasing anything larger than this." He laid the hare beside the pile of sticks and sat down, folding his knees to one side.

Timoken didn't ask how the wizard had managed to catch the hare. He didn't want to know. He disliked hunting and killing creatures he could talk to.

"You won't have to catch another hare," he told the wizard.

"How so?"

"Because I can . . ."

Eri raised an eyebrow. "Don't tell me you can conjure meat from the sky."

"No. I can multiply."

"Multiply?" The wizard pondered the word for a while before saying, "That is quite an accomplishment."

The wizard's nephew, Edern, had told Timoken that Eri could light a fire with his fingers. This was also one of Timoken's talents, but he was interested to see how the wizard would do it. When tiny flames began to lick the dry twigs, Eri said, "I might have left my bag of tricks behind, but I still have a few up my sleeve."

"What is in your bag of tricks?" asked Timoken.

"Some potions," the wizard said airily. "Herbs, of course, and also bats and toads, dragonflies and snakes."

"Dead?"

"Of course, dead. Dry as parchment. I have some fish teeth, too."

"Fish teeth?" Timoken was impressed. "In all my years of traveling I never saw a fish tooth."

"No?" The wizard smiled as flames roared to the top of Timoken's pile of sticks. "Believe me, fish teeth are very potent, and I'm sorry to lose them. No matter. We will find more." Eri nodded at the beach. "Right here, if I'm not mistaken." He began to skin the hare.

The meat tasted good, Timoken had to admit. He took a few pieces of the cooked hare and, turning his back on the wizard, discreetly multiplied them.

"We cannot survive on hare meat," Eri said gently. "Winter is coming and we shall need hides to keep us warm, leather for our feet, for carrying water, for our roof, for everything."

Keeping his back turned, Timoken picked up the hare's skin and lightly ran his hands across it. Then he murmured a wishing prayer in his own language, and within minutes, the hareskin had become a pile of soft furs. Gathering them in his arms, Timoken turned to the wizard. "There," he said. "We shall be as warm as bears."

"We shall indeed, boy." Eri laughed. "But you'll have to forgive me if I do a little hunting of my own."

Timoken noticed that Gabar had wandered off. He could hear

the camel shaking branches and munching dry leaves. It was getting dark and Timoken didn't want to lose sight of his camel. He was about to go after him when Gabar trotted out of the shadows.

"Strangers," said the camel.

"Strangers?" said Timoken. "Animals? Humans?"

"In trees," Gabar replied.

"Birds?" Timoken ventured.

"In the trees," the camel repeated. "Not birds."

"What are you both bellowing about?" asked the wizard.

"My camel says there are strangers in the trees," said Timoken.

The wizard sucked his teeth. "Not much we can do about it. We don't have a lantern."

"We have this." Timoken pulled a long stick from the edge of the fire. Only the tip glowed red. Wrapping dried leaves and grass around the stick, Timoken ran into the trees. With a leap, he was in the air. Flying through the higher branches, he waved his stick. The smoldering leaves, fanned by the air, burst into flame. In their wavering light, Timoken thought he saw a glistening eye, a face, a foot, but he couldn't be sure.

"What are you?" he called. "Come out!" He tried the birdcalls that he knew and thought he heard a whisper, a rustle. But, again, he couldn't be sure.

When he returned to the clearing Timoken told Eri that whoever, or whatever, it was might have been afraid of a flying boy. "I don't think they mean us any harm," he said. "If they had weapons, they could have killed me."

"Your camel is a nervous creature," said Eri. "He sees things that are not there."

"Maybe." Timoken glanced at Gabar, feeling he'd betrayed the camel.

The camel observed the doubt in Eri's eyes. "I know what I saw," Gabar grunted, settling himself behind the boy.

Timoken stroked the camel's neck. "I don't doubt you, Gabar."

The camel sighed and closed his eyes.

Eri banked up the fire. He yawned and stretched out his pale, bony legs before the flames. Timoken frowned at the bruises covering the wizard's shins.

"Osbern's men did their worst," Eri muttered. "But my legs can still carry me. Tomorrow I'll find plants and cure my bruises."

Timoken thought of offering his cloak. It might ease the old man's pain. But he didn't want to belittle the wizard's own skills.

They sat in silence for a while, with only the crackle of flames to disturb their thoughts. And then Eri said, "My nephew told me a little of your history, but I would like to hear it from your own lips."

Timoken squeezed his eyes tight shut. Sometimes he tried to blot the worst memories out of his head, but he had never succeeded, and he had come to realize that they would always be with him, they were part of him as much as his legs or his arms, or his black, woolly hair.

"Your memories cause you pain, boy," said Eri. "Better to share them."

Timoken opened his eyes. "Perhaps you're right." Clenching his fists, he told the wizard about his early years in a secret African kingdom. With a smile on his face, he described a beautiful place of warm, green forests; clear streams teeming with fish; of orchards full of fruit; and a sky that was always blue. The pain of the outside world was unknown, and never intruded.

"And then THEY found us." Timoken took a breath. For a moment it seemed as if he would never let it out again.

"They?" prompted the wizard.

"Beings from the dark underside of the forest. Greenish things with red eyes and hair like vines. Their bones are soft, their hands like roots. They are called viridees." Timoken shuddered. "Their leader . . . their leader . . ." For a moment he couldn't say the words, and then, speaking fast and lowering his eyes, he told the wizard how his father, the king, had been killed by the lord of the viridees.

"He cut off my father's head." Timoken buried his face in his hands. "We saw it all, my sister and I, from the roof of the palace. But before the viridees came with their knives and sabers, my mother put this crown on my head and I have never been able to take it off." He drew his cloak closer around his shoulders. "And then she gave me the web of the last moon spider. She said it would protect me, and she also told me that I could fly."

"You didn't know until that moment?" asked the wizard in surprise.

"I was happy. I had no need to fly."

Eri nodded. "I see. And where is the spider's web?"

"Here." Timoken lifted a corner of his red cloak. "I turned it into a cloak. My mother also gave me a bottle containing Alixir, the water of life. The moment I left the secret kingdom, the viridees tried to kill me, and steal the cloak and the bottle. But viridees can't survive in the cold, so I'm safe here, in Britain, as far as I know."

"And how long have you been traveling, little king?" asked the wizard.

"You might find this difficult to believe." Timoken looked away from Eri's penetrating gaze. "But I left the secret kingdom over two hundred years ago. The water of life kept me and my sister young. We took one drop of the Alixir every new moon, and so did Gabar." He smiled and patted his camel's back. "Zobayda wore a ring that protected us, but the viridees lured her away, and for many years we were apart. I only found my sister a year ago, after I met your nephew, Edern. He'd just escaped from his kidnappers and fallen into a deep ravine. I lost the water of life when I rescued him, or I should say that Gabar lost it when he fell into the river below. It was in a bag strapped to his back."

"Edern." The wizard shook his head. "You are his greatest friend. He will miss you. But tell me, Timoken, what happened to your mother?"

"My mother?" This was a part of his story that always made Timoken feel guilty. "She was on the palace roof when I flew into the air with my sister. I looked down and my mother was gone, hidden by a mass of black-robed soldiers. Maybe I could have rescued her, too. Why didn't she hold on to me? I've never stopped wondering."

"Perhaps she was afraid of holding you back," the wizard said gently. "For her, you and your sister were the future. You were safe. That's all she needed to know."

Timoken stared at the wizard, repeating the old man's words in his head. He began to feel lighter, as though something heavy had been lifted away from him. And then his thoughts turned to Mabon and the weight came down again. *Have I killed my friend? Is he alive or dead?* Timoken curled up beside his camel and the animal's quiet heartbeat gradually lulled him to sleep.

The wizard gazed at the fire. He threw another bundle of twigs onto the dying flames and they roared to life. Timoken's story had unsettled him. There were beings in the northern forest, too. Here they were not called viridees, they had another name. A name the wizard wouldn't allow himself to utter, even in a whisper. Suppose they could connect?

"Unthinkable," muttered Eri. Pulling a pile of fur on top of himself, he lay down beside the fire. On the other side of the flames, Timoken smiled in his sleep.

"What now, little king?" the wizard murmured. And then he, too, fell asleep.

The fire burned steadily for a while, and then it began to die. When it was just a pile of glowing embers, the camel woke up. THEY were coming, just as he had guessed they would.

A cloud of stars fell gently through the trees. The camel blinked. No, they were not stars. Now he could see that the lights came from the tips of long rushes held by children. They were not falling from the trees, but descending on thin creepers. Children usually made a noise, but these slight creatures were completely silent. The camel was too surprised to utter a sound.

When every child was down, they began to move toward the glade. They came from all sides: thin, wiry children with tanned, roughened skin. Their long hair was wild and matted and they wore ill-fitting garments patched with fur and feathers and held together with strings of creeper. They were rebels' children from the town of Innswood. Two years ago, the people of Innswood had revolted against the conquerors' laws. The result was inevitable. Soldiers came in the night. Houses were burned, men and women captured or killed. The children ran into the trees to hide.

The forest was home to more than thirty children now. They had built shelters in the trees and learned to keep silent, though sometimes, in the evenings, they would speak in whispers, telling one another their stories: how they had hidden in baskets

and boxes, in cowsheds and cauldrons, while the conquerors rav-
aged their homes.

They tried to help one another, to share the hares and squir-
rels and pigeons they caught, the nuts and berries they found,
the snakes and beetles and roots. But when there wasn't enough,
fighting would break out. It was always the younger ones who
suffered.

The children crept forward. Closer and closer. Holding their
rush-lights high, they formed a circle, five deep, around the boy,
the old man, and the magic beast. All at once, the beast made a
noise like something from the underworld, the boy woke up, and
the children leaped away. Some forgot to be silent and let out
hoots of fear.

"Who are you?" asked Timoken, drawing his cloak tight
around himself.

The children stared at him. They hardly moved a muscle.

The wizard had also woken up. He rubbed his eyes and
looked around the circle of children. He guessed who they were.
Rebels' children. He had heard of a rebellion in the north.

"What d'you want?" Timoken asked the children. "Are you
hungry?" They certainly looked it.

The children had learned never to trust a stranger. They

whispered among themselves and frowned at the camel. They had never seen anyone with skin as dark as Timoken's.

"Rebels' children," Eri muttered. "They've done well to survive in the wild."

One of the girls suddenly stepped forward. "I am Elfrieda." She spoke defiantly, her head held high as though her dress of fur and feathers were a fine robe edged in gold. Her thick, matted hair covered her shoulders like a rug of muddy sheepskin.

"I am Timoken, and this is Eri, the wizard." Timoken indicated the old man. "And this is Gabar, my camel." He patted the camel's neck.

"Camel," said Elfrieda, frowning.

"Camel," whispered one of the children. Others repeated it and the whispered word traveled around the group like a great rustling of leaves.

Whether Gabar understood or not, he suddenly got to his feet and gave another loud bellow.

The children fell silent. They stared at the magic beast in awe, and then a voice said, "He is mighty ugly."

Timoken stared into the crowd. It made him angry to hear Gabar being called ugly. But he knew that a camel was strange to Northern people.

"Who said my camel was ugly?" he demanded.

There was no answer. Elfrieda lifted her chin and said haugh-
tily, "You can't say he's beautiful."

"I do," Timoken replied.

"There," said the wizard. "I might not agree with my young
friend, but that camel is a marvel."

The crowd of children murmured among themselves. One of
them grumbled and stepped back, pushing another sideways.
Others began to mutter and complain, and then the cause of all
the grumbling, a very small boy, crawled out of the crowd, stood
up, and went over to Gabar. He gazed at the camel, his brown
eyes shining. Gabar appeared not to notice the boy, so far beneath
him, but all at once he lowered his neck and the boy gently
stroked him.

"Karli, get away from that thing." It was the voice of the boy
who had called Gabar ugly.

The little boy took no notice.

"The camel won't hurt him," said Timoken.

"But I will." A tall boy pushed his way past the other children. His blond curls were matted with dust and his wide face
scarred with scratches. He was bigger than Timoken, and his
voice had begun to break.

"Are you his brother?" asked Timoken, looking at the small
boy, whose hair was a dark oak-brown.

"Do I look like his brother?" said the tall boy with a sneer. "I am Thorkil and I am his protector."

"He's your slave, you mean," muttered a quiet voice.

Interesting, thought Timoken. They were not an entirely happy group. He wasn't sure that he wanted to be part of their quarreling.

Either Thorkil hadn't heard the quiet voice, or he chose to ignore it. "Karli, come here!" He strode up to the small boy and grabbed his arm.

Timoken could have chosen to believe that Thorkil was Karli's protector and allowed him to drag the little boy away. But the quiet voice in the crowd had alerted him.

"Let it rest, Timoken," Eri warned.

It was too late. Timoken's hand was already on Thorkil's shoulder. "Leave him alone."

"What did you say?" Eyes blazing, Thorkil swung around and pulled a dagger from his belt.

Just as swiftly, Timoken sank his fingers into Thorkil's wrist and the dagger dropped to the ground.

Thorkil stared at Timoken. "So your fingers can burn, stranger." He spoke in a low voice, full of hatred. "But you had better watch out, because I never forget."

CHAPTER 4
A Magic Beast

The wizard could still move faster than most, in spite of his bruises. He placed himself between the two boys before either could do any harm.

"We are all victims of the conquerors," Eri said sternly. "We must keep our wits about us if we are to survive."

"I need my dagger." Thorkil glared at the wizard, whose foot rested on the blade.

"Give me your word that you won't use it," Eri demanded.

Thorkil's gray eyes narrowed. The wizard could see that honor still meant something to this arrogant boy.

"How can I live without a blade?" Thorkil said sullenly. "How can I hunt, eat, and make the things I need?"

"You know very well what I mean," Eri replied. "Give me your word that you won't use your dagger to harm anyone here."

Timoken noticed that Elfrieda had been anxiously watching Thorkil, and now she said, "So my brother is not allowed to defend himself?"

"I am sure that no one here wished him any harm." Eri stepped off the dagger and picked it up. "Your word, boy!" he said.

Thorkil remained silent, his brow creased. He seemed to be struggling to remember something, and then out it came. "On the blood of my father, Earl Sigurd of Holfingel, I give my solemn promise that I will not use my weapon against anyone here present."

Timoken was impressed. He hadn't expected such a long and solemn oath.

Eri was also surprised by Thorkil's words. He handed over the dagger and watched the boy push it into his belt.

"And now perhaps you will allow us to get some sleep," said the wizard. "The sun will soon be up, and Timoken and I have a long journey to make."

Do we? thought Timoken. He had hoped they might stay here

for a while. But perhaps these wild-looking children didn't want strangers in their patch of forest.

Led by Thorkil, the children moved back into the trees. Timoken watched them effortlessly skim up the creepers, the rush-lights held in their teeth. When they reached the lower branches, they pulled the creepers up into the trees. The silence that followed made it seem as though the appearance of the children had been just a dream.

The next morning there was no sign of the children. Timoken thought he might fly up into the trees and find them, but he decided against it. If they wanted to be seen, they would appear soon enough. "Are you determined to move on?" he asked the wizard.

"I think it best," said Eri.

They stamped out the last embers of the fire and led Gabar back to the beach. As soon as his feet touched the sand, the camel gathered speed and began to gallop. Timoken let him go and watched him running, turning, and bellowing for joy.

"I hope this won't go on too long," Eri said anxiously. "It might take us all day to find a safe place to rest."

"We're safe already," said Timoken.

"I doubt it." Eri looked toward the cliffs that rose on one side of the beach. "The conquerors have spies everywhere. Even as we speak, someone could be watching us."

Timoken followed his gaze. He saw only white seabirds tilting beside the cliffs or resting on the rocky ledges and calling into the wind. At the top of the cliffs, a few stunted trees grew among the clumps of golden gorse. And high above it all, a vigilant eagle soared, watching its prey. Timoken thought of Edern, who had chosen an eagle to be his emblem because it was as near as he could get to flying.

"Eri, will I ever see Edern again?" asked Timoken. "I want to know if I'll see my friends, Mabon, Peredur, and Gereint. And I can't bear to think I'll never see my sister, Zobayda, again. In the many years when we were apart she couldn't take the water of life and so she has aged much faster than me."

The wizard pursed his lips. He licked his forefinger and held it in the air. "Southwest," he murmured. "A kindly wind, but sometimes wet." Turning to Timoken, he said, "I don't have an answer for you, but perhaps I'll try and dream one if we get some peace."

"Thank you." Timoken knew that Eri was a great wizard. Answers were a favor and he shouldn't ask for too many. Yet there was someone he hadn't mentioned, someone he hadn't seen for a while, but whose memory was as fresh as though she were sitting before him at that very moment.

The wizard bunched the top of his cloak around his neck and rubbed his hands. He gave Timoken a thoughtful smile and said, "I believe you would also like to know about that girl who came with you from Castile. Her name escapes me."

"Berenice," Timoken said shyly. "She's being kept with the women, learning to play the harp and other womanly things."

"She's a beautiful girl. Even without a dowry, she will be much in demand. Osbern will guard her like his treasures." Eri hesitated and then continued solemnly, "It is possible that one day you will see your friends again, and even your sister, who is a mature lady now. But as for Berenice, it is likely that she will be married very soon, and beyond your reach forever."

Timoken frowned up at the clouds. "Married? But we belong together, and I thought . . . Would she want to marry a rich lord, Eri? A conqueror with a castle of his own? Maybe she would. But I can build a castle as fine as any prince's."

"I'm sorry, Timoken," Eri said gently. "That would take time, and it may be too late."

"But will you try and bring her into your dreams?"

"I will," said the wizard.

Timoken called Gabar, and the camel reluctantly came over to him. Timoken tied his bundle of hare's skins onto the saddle, saying, "We must travel again, Gabar."

"Where now, Family?" asked the camel. "Can we look for more sand?"

Timoken smiled. "We'll try," he said. "Now, let the wizard climb onto your back. He can't fly like me."

The camel knelt while his passengers climbed onto their lumpy seat. A low, continuous grumble came from the wizard as Gabar stood up, and Timoken couldn't help laughing.

"It's all very well for you," said Eri, "but my bottom is nothing but bone, and even covered with furs, a hump is the most uncomfortable thing I have ever sat on."

"I'll make a proper saddle when we reach . . ." Timoken hesitated. "Where are we going, Eri?"

"Into the wild north. Let your camel find the route."

"Come, Gabar," Timoken said to the camel. "Up above the cliffs and into the clouds. Away from the sun and into the wilderness."

Sand, thought Gabar. *More sand.* He walked happily across the beach until he felt Timoken tug the hair on his back, and then he began to rise into the air.

At the edge of the trees, a boy and a girl stood watching the camel walk across the vast stretch of sand. They watched until the magic beast was hardly more than a distant form bobbing beside the incoming tide, and they gasped as the creature slowly rose into the air.

Their mouths agape, the children ran onto the sand and watched the camel lift his passengers into the sky. Once there, he hovered a moment before slowly turning and flying back toward the children. When he passed over their heads, they could clearly see his long brown neck and the knobbly forelegs stretched out before him.

The girl, Sila, waited until the camel was out of sight. Then, clutching the small boy's shoulder, she said, "Karli, the others won't believe us. So don't bother to tell them what we've seen."

Karli vehemently shook his head. "Never. It's our secret, Sila."

It was Sila whose quiet voice had alerted Timoken. She was the only one brave enough to speak out against Thorkil. His treatment of Karli and the other small children made her angry. Thorkil might be an earl's son, but now he was no better than the rest of the tree children. They were all the same; they had nothing to live on but their wits.

"Sila, let's follow them," said Karli.

"Follow? But we can't, they're in the sky."

"The magic beast likes sand." Karli tugged her arm. "I could see how he danced on it. He was so happy."

Sila laughed. "Beasts don't dance."

"Magic beasts do. You saw him."

Sila nodded. "Yes, I saw him."

"Let's go, then. We'll walk beside the sea until we find another beach and, one day, there they'll be: the magic beast, the wizard, and the boy who wanted to help me."

"I think he's a king," Sila said thoughtfully.

"A king?" Karli clapped his hands. "Let's find him."

Without their noticing, a small crowd had crept up behind them.

"What's all the excitement?" asked a boy wearing sealskin breeches.

"We saw—" Karli began excitedly.

Sila shot him a warning glance and said, "The strangers have gone—riding their magic beast."

"We're going to follow them," said Karli.

The boy in sealskin breeches shook his head, grinning. "You won't get far. Which way did they go?"

Karli twirled around in the sand, waving his arms about,

while Sila watched him anxiously. "That way," he said at last, pointing at the trees.

"Back into the forest?" asked a girl, frowning. "We didn't see them."

"Because they're magic," Karli told her.

The boy in the sealskin breeches looked concerned. "Don't go, Sila. It's not safe to travel alone, just the two of you."

"Then come with us, Tumi," cried Karli.

"What's going on here?" Thorkil strode up to them. He was followed by a gang of teenage boys carrying roughly made spears.

"We were judging the tide," Tumi said quickly. "It might be right for fishing."

"Ah, going to catch supper are you, fisher boy?" Thorkil said in a condescending tone. "Where's your net?"

"I forgot it." Tumi turned away from Thorkil, afraid that he'd sounded too bold.

"I forgot it," mimicked Thorkil, and the group behind him laughed. But all too soon Thorkil's tone changed. He had caught sight of Karli and, striding forward, he grabbed hold of the little boy's arm. "Where's your needle?" he demanded. "Why aren't you mending my jerkin?"

"The bone needle is too sharp, it hurts his fingers," said Sila. "Look at them." She held up Karli's hand, so they could all see the scars and the torn skin on his palm and fingers.

Thorkil laughed scornfully. "I have scars on my feet, on my arms, and here"—he touched his cheek—"on my face. Life is hard. We all have scars, but we must put up with them."

Sila stared defiantly at Thorkil for a moment, and then she dropped her gaze and let go of Karli's hand.

"Back to work, everyone." Thorkil turned away and marched into the trees. He was followed by his gang, who began to bicker and shove as they tried to pass one another on the narrow track.

Sila sighed. A long day of running in useless circles lay ahead. A day of wading through thorns and falling in thickets, losing her bark shoes, and staining her hands and face with berries. There had to be a better way to survive.

Tumi looked back at her. "I'll catch a fish today, Sila." He gave her one of his mischievous, twisty smiles. "We won't go hungry, I promise you."

"Good luck, Tumi." Sila returned his smile. "It's about time we had some real food."

Karli ran up behind her. Catching her hand, he whispered, "Shall we go, Sila? Shall we go and find the magic beast?"

Sila nodded. "Perhaps."

"Please, Sila? Can we go tonight, after Tumi's fish? I don't want to live here anymore."

"Nor do I, Karli. But we must think and plan. Be patient."

"I can't." Karli's small face looked desperately earnest. "I'm going tonight. I'll go alone if I have to."

CHAPTER 5
The Widows' Tower

Castle Melyntha had four towers. One of them was known as the Widows' Tower, even though there were young, unmarried women living there.

Girls of high rank were sent to the Widows' Tower at the age of twelve. There, among other skills, they learned to embroider and play the harp. Their teachers were widows, some not yet twenty, who had lost their husbands on the battlefield. Most of the older widows were strict and stone-faced, though there were a few who liked to laugh, and looking into their eyes, you could tell that they still longed for excitement.

Timoken's sister, Zobayda, was like none of the others. She told fabulous tales of the life she had led in Africa, and later with her husband, Tariq, the toy maker. She still kept a bag filled with the beautiful toys he had made.

The Widows' Tower was not a prison, but single women of rank were not expected to wander alone in the castle grounds. The tower was a place for learning how to be a good wife. When Beri came to Britain with Timoken and his sister, she had hoped for freedom. Instead, she had been sent to this dreary tower. Zobayda explained that if she were to survive, this was the life she must accept, any other would be dangerous — unthinkable. For Beri, rules were meant to be broken. Dressed as a boy, she would often slip away from the tower and meet Timoken and Edern beneath the trees in the castle orchard.

Beri's father had been the bravest and best swordsman in all of Spain. He had taught his daughter how to use the sword, and she could hold her own against most young men. Timoken had been aware of this. He had made an enchanted sword for her, but she was not permitted to wear it hanging from her fine jeweled belt. So the enchanted sword lay in a wooden chest, where the older widows could keep an eye on it. Beri knew exactly the moments when the chest was left unguarded.

The widows in the tower insisted on using her full name, Berenice. Beri preferred the shortened version. She knew she was being prepared for marriage. Some of the girls left the tower soon

after their fourteenth birthdays. Beri wondered about the husbands they might have. Were they old and wrinkled? Were they
knights, or were they fat and greasy councillors? She couldn't
bring herself to imagine her own fate.

She decided that she must leave Castle Melyntha and search
for a better future. Perhaps she could persuade Timoken and the
four Britons to go with her?

The servant girl Mair often brought news to the tower. A few
hours after Timoken's escape, Mair came to the girls' chamber,
where Beri stood alone, gazing out the window.

"Did you hear the guards?" Mair laid a clean dress on one of
the beds. "Your friend Timoken has escaped."

"Escaped?" Beri was puzzled. "How so? He was free to come
and go as he wished."

Mair solemnly shook her head. "No. They put him in prison."

"Why?" asked Beri, astonished.

"He killed Mabon, the archer."

"Impossible!" Beri furiously paced about the chamber, shaking her head. "Mabon was Timoken's friend. They were like
this." She linked her fingers so tightly together that the knuck-
les showed white.

"I know," Mair agreed. "It's a mystery. They say that Mabon
was killed with an arrow, but the African has never used a bow."

Beri sank onto the bed. "Something is very, very wrong. The prince would never put Timoken in that dreadful cell."

"There's talk..." Mair faltered and tears filled her eyes. "They say that Prince Griffith is dead. Sir Osbern holds the castle now. Some of the Britons speak of leaving. They believe that soon the castle will be filled with the conquerors' men."

Beri stared at Mair. "What will it mean for us, Mair? You and me?"

Mair shrugged. "Welsh Britons, like me, will have the worse time of it. As for you, Lady Berenice, I think Sir Osbern might start locking this tower, and you'll all be prisoners, like Timoken, though in more comfortable surroundings. If I were you, I'd try and go, soon as you can. Though I can't advise where."

One of the widows called to Mair and, rolling her eyes at Beri, she ran off, whispering, "Go soon."

For several minutes Beri sat perfectly still, puzzling, wondering, trying to make sense of everything she'd heard.

"Zobayda will know what to do," she told herself. "We'll go together."

It was the possession of toys that had persuaded the other widows that Zobayda should have care of the baby. No one knew where he came from. One morning a soldier appeared at the door to the Widows' Tower and handed the baby to a servant. "It's to grow here till it's three years" was all he said.

The baby was a boy. It was rumored that he was the son of a Welsh Briton, but who knew? His mother was dead, obviously. And perhaps his father, too. The baby's eyes were a dark, stormy gray. He was now a year old and he had grown to love Zobayda. He wouldn't be parted from her. She called him Tariq, after her husband. But, of course, that couldn't have been the name his parents had chosen for him.

Beri went to her small window. Below her lay the forest, its bright autumn canopy fading to dull gold in the distant morning mist.

Where was Timoken now? Could she and Zobayda find him?

Beri had a sudden thought. She had forgotten the baby. They would have to take him with them. But could a baby survive such a journey? It might take many weeks, and who knew what dangers lay in the vast, wild forest?

CHAPTER 6
Deadly Sands

Eri had fallen asleep, his head resting between Timoken's shoulder blades, his bony hands locked together around the boy's waist. Even in sleep, the wizard had an iron grip.

Frost began to edge into the wind. Timoken shivered. *We must descend soon*, he thought, *or we'll fall to earth like blocks of ice.* The image amused him and he chuckled to himself. "Down soon, Gabar," he shouted into the wind.

"Here!" Gabar began to drop through the cold air.

Timoken looked down. He saw a great stretch of milk-white land. Gabar was swiftly falling toward it. It was sand, for it was bordered on one side by the sea. But there was something ominous about the vast, pale sweep.

"Not here, Gabar," said Timoken, tugging at the reins.

"Here," Gabar grunted defiantly.

"No. There's something wrong."

"It's sand," the camel argued. "I long for it. I *will* go down."

"No, Gabar!" Timoken gave an angry bellow.

The wizard woke up. "What's happening?" he grumbled.

"We're descending," Timoken shouted over his shoulder. "Gabar wants sand, but I don't trust the land beneath us."

Eri squinted down at the bleached sweep of earth. "Stop your mulish creature," he cried. "We've reached the Deadly Sands. They will swallow us."

"Swallow?" yelled Timoken, tugging at the hair on Gabar's back. "Gabar, do you want to be eaten by the earth?"

"Sand," said the camel stubbornly, "is always good." He dropped again.

"No!" Timoken looked down. Almost luminescent against the dark sea, the sand seemed to beckon, to draw them in like a magnet. "Believe me, Gabar. Have I ever lied to you?"

"No, Family," the camel admitted. He struggled in the air for a moment, kicking out his legs and twisting his head. "The sand calls me," he moaned regretfully, "and I can't escape it."

The camel dropped again and the deadly beach rushed toward them.

Timoken could sense how his camel battled the draw of the

sand. He tugged helplessly at the shaggy back, but it was like trying to lift a thousand camels. And then it came to him, almost too late. Tearing the moon cloak from his shoulders, he threw it over the camel's head.

"Now you can't see the sand, Gabar," he said. "There is no sand, and it can't call you."

"I'm blind," bellowed the camel.

"Climb, Gabar, climb!" yelled Timoken.

He felt the camel's muscles ripple, heard a grunt of defiance. A huge heartbeat throbbed through Gabar's body and slowly, very slowly, he lifted away from the Deadly Sands.

"On now, Gabar. Onward, and I'll let you see again." Timoken patted the shaggy back.

Gabar galloped into the sky, rolling his head this way and that, trying to rid himself of his blindfold. Frantically, he climbed his way upward, higher and higher, until the moon cloak slipped from his head and fell into Timoken's arms. But still the camel climbed, his great foreteet treading the wind, while the wizard moaned and grunted, sinking his nails into Timoken's shoulders until he bruised the skin.

Timoken gritted his teeth and let the camel continue to climb a moment longer before crying, "No higher, Gabar, or we'll freeze to death."

"Where, then?" snorted the camel. "Ice or sand?"

Hoping they had passed over the white beach, Timoken said, "There are many places between ice and sand, Gabar. You can fly lower now."

"I hope you're instructing the creature to descend," grumbled Eri. "I'm likely to become an ice man very soon."

"Take this," Timoken passed his cloak to the wizard.

Eri looked doubtfully at the cloak, before wrapping it around his own cloak. "Shivering stars," he breathed. "This flimsy cloak is as warm as sheepskin. What's it made of?"

His words were lost in the wind as Gabar, suddenly blown sideways, plummeted through the clouds. To Timoken's relief, a rusty-colored headland appeared beneath them.

"Here, Gabar," Timoken shouted. "Let's go down."

The camel's descent was so swift, Eri, caught off guard, found his legs flying out behind him. "Slower," he screeched, his bony fingers now biting into Timoken's waist. But the camel's feet were already skimming a field of bracken. Gabar pawed the earth with one foot, then another, absorbing the shock of a sudden landing. He was now an expert at those.

They found themselves on a high finger of land, jutting out into the dark sea. Far below, the waves crashed and slapped against the rocks.

The first stars were beginning to show, and a thin splinter of light sliced through the darkening sky: the new moon. For more than two hundred years, whenever the new moon appeared, Timoken had sipped a drop of Alixir from a bird-shaped bottle; the liquid came from a moonlit pool deep in the African forest, and the jinni who had made Timoken's cloak had also cast a spell on the moonlit water, transforming it into the water of life.

"I see the new moon," grunted Gabar.

"I see it, too," said Timoken.

"Where is the bottle?" Gabar's memory was not perfect.

Timoken sighed. "I've told you a hundred times. We lost it when you fell into the river."

The wizard had started wading through the bracken. He had seen a small stand of trees in the distance. Looking back at Timoken, he shouted, "What are you two whispering about?"

"A camel couldn't whisper even if it wanted to." Timoken laughed, running to catch up with Eri.

"Hmph!" the wizard grunted. "How should I know?"

They spent the night beneath the trees. All three were so weary, they barely had time to light a fire before they fell asleep. Timoken shyly offered the wizard a place beneath his cloak, and Eri eagerly accepted.

When they woke up, they found they were on a hilltop that

sloped gently down to a wide valley of autumn trees. There was not a wisp of smoke to show the presence of another human, nor a sound, except for the calling of eagles and a soft animal rustling in the bracken.

"It's like a new land," said Timoken. "Perhaps we can stay here. We're far from the conquerors now."

Eri looked doubtful. "Not far enough," he said.

"I'll go into the forest and look for signs," Timoken said eagerly.

"Without a weapon?" Eri shook his head.

Timoken had been unable to reach his sword and shield before their flight from the castle. He would have to make another. But not yet.

"Don't worry, Eri. I can defend myself." Timoken ran down the hill. The air was crisp, the sky a bright frosty blue. He felt invincible. When he reached the first line of trees, he looked back and saw the wizard standing in the field of bracken. The sleeves of his earth-brown robe fluttered in the wind, and a hood covered his head. Timoken couldn't see the wizard's eyes, and yet he felt the weight of the man's gaze on him. He lifted a hand, but Eri remained motionless. With a little shiver of apprehension, Timoken let his hand fall to his side and ran into the trees.

It was an ancient forest. The oaks, broad with age, bore leaves the color of bronze. Some of the trees had died and lay where they had fallen, maybe a thousand years ago. Tiny creatures darted through the gleaming moss that covered the bark, and the dark, rotting wood bristled with life. The constant fluttering and calling of birds filled the soft air.

Timoken knew that no one had walked here for many hundreds of years. He took off his shoes, to feel the footsteps far beneath the earth. *Who had been the first?* he thought. *Who were they, the people who had once stepped through the forest? No conqueror had set foot on this rich earth, no Saxon. Perhaps not even the Britons' ancestors.*

Whoever they were, their spirits seemed to welcome Timoken, the boy from Africa. He began to run. Spreading his arms and using every animal language he knew, he called to the creatures of the forest.

"I have found you, my home," he sang. And he thought of his brave mother who, before she died, had told him that, one day, he would find a new home.

Timoken lay on a fallen tree and sank his hands into the deep moss at his side. *Somewhere here I'll build a home for us,* he thought. *For me and Eri and all my friends, and we'll be safe.*

What about Mabon? said a voice in his head. He couldn't answer that.

He rolled off the tree and walked on until he found a wild, tumbling river. On the other side, a red cliff reached high above the trees. Timoken flew up to the cliff top and looked west, expecting to see the ocean, but he saw only trees sweeping to the horizon. How far had he come? He leaped from the cliff and flew above the forest for a while.

A chill in the air sent him down to the forest for warmth. But the sun had gone and a cold mist was beginning to seep from the earth. Timoken felt a light touch on his cheek, a tiny droplet of freezing water. When he tried to draw his cloak tight around himself, he was aware of a slight tug, as though someone was pulling at it from behind. But there was no one there. And then, from the corner of his eye, he glimpsed a pale shape drifting through the trees beside him; another followed it. He turned his head and saw a dull light gliding between distant branches. Timoken began to run.

It was almost dark when Timoken left the forest. In the bag at his waist, he carried nuts and berries for his camel and the wizard. As he walked through the bracken, he could see Gabar dozing at the edge of the trees.

"I've got food for you, Gabar," cried Timoken, running up to his camel.

"I've had plenty. Where've you been?" Gabar grunted reproachfully.

"In our new kingdom." Timoken crouched beside the camel. "It's a fine place, Gabar. And I'll build a castle to keep us all safe."

"Any sand?" enquired the camel.

"Perhaps," Timoken said uncertainly.

"Perhaps," echoed the camel. He yawned, lowered his head, and emitted a grumpy sigh.

Timoken stood up and patted the camel's neck. "I'll make sand if I have to," he assured him.

He had expected to find the wizard under the trees, wrapped in his cloak and sleeping. But there was no sign of him.

"Where's Eri?" Timoken asked the camel.

"Gone," said Gabar.

"Where?" Timoken looked anxiously over his shoulder.

"He didn't tell me." Gabar would never admit to a failure of understanding.

"Of course not," Timoken said quickly. He gazed at the field of bracken, his eyes roaming along the edge of the forest. Night was falling. No doubt Eri had found somewhere safe to sleep.

The warm hollow of a tree, perhaps. He was a wizard, after all, and had the means to look after himself.

Timoken lit a fire and sat a moment, staring into the flames. In spite of the sinister beings in the forest, the certainty that he had found his place in the world was stronger than ever. . . .

He could picture how it would be: he and his friends, together again, sitting before a great fire in their new home. Safe from Osbern, safe from Stenulf and Aelfric. And then he thought of Mabon, and the bright picture was shattered. What would Osbern do to Mabon when he discovered he was still alive, after failing to kill an African who might be a king? His eyes began to close. Just before he fell asleep, he found himself murmuring, "Eri, where are you?"

Timoken was still asleep when the camel woke up and went in search of water. He found a stream and drank thirstily. The grass on the bank had a light dusting of frost, but Gabar was used to the cold. That didn't mean he liked it. Nor did he like the damp bracken that brushed his knees. He thought of the great beach of sand that lay just to the south of the headland. He longed for it. Just one quick look, he thought, to savor the memory, to imagine the feel of dry sand beneath his feet.

Why not? thought Gabar. *Why not take a look?* He was running through the bracken now, happiness flooding his body.

Soon he would see the thing he loved. He stopped, just in time, at the edge of the cliff. He trembled with shock. For he might have fallen. Without Timoken, he couldn't fly. It was the boy who kept him aloft. Without his family, Gabar was just an extremely long-lived camel.

Gabar gazed at the vast bay in astonishment. Gone was the pale sand. It had vanished under a swirling blanket of water.

Swallowed, thought Gabar. *It is like my family said. The sand has been swallowed.*

Not all the sand had gone, however. Small banks of higher ground were still visible, but, encircled by the rushing tide, these, too, were slowly being swallowed.

On one of the sandbanks there were two dots. Gabar's lashes fluttered in a long blink. Something was wrong. Those dots should not be there. They were human beings and soon they would be swallowed, too. The camel bellowed. Strands of spittle flew from his mouth. He backed away from the edge of the cliff, wheeled around, and ran to his family.

CHAPTER 7
Half-Ear and Worm-Apple

Sila woke up. It was pitch-dark in the tree-hide. She could hear the soft breathing of the others, all around her, and then something else: a quiet rustling. It came from the corner where Karli slept.

"Karli?" she whispered. "What are you doing?"

"I'm going," he said.

"Not now. It's dark. The moon is too slight."

"I can see by the stars. And I know where they've gone, the boy and his camel. They'll follow the sand."

"You can't go alone. I'm coming with you." Sila pushed her few possessions into a straw bag: her mother's bone comb; a blanket; a string of shells; a wooden platter; a long, sharp flint; a clay cup; a spoon; and several rushes, ready to light.

"I'm glad you're coming, Sila," Karli whispered.

They crawled out of the hide and Sila let down the creeper. One end was tied to a stump in the wide mesh of branches that held their tree-home. Sila slipped her arm through a loop of string attached to her bag. Holding tight to the creeper, she swung her legs down until she could feel the vine between her feet.

"Wait till I'm there and I'll hold it steady for you." She spoke so softly that Karli didn't hear her. He began to follow while she was still swinging down.

"No, Karli," she hissed.

But Karli couldn't wait. He wanted to run before his feet touched the earth. He wanted to be gone.

"Who's there?" said a voice, not Karli's.

"Hush!" Sila quietly silenced Karli.

She jumped to the ground and the little boy tumbled beside her.

Tumi peered into the dark beneath him. He couldn't see the children but he knew who they were. He felt for the creeper and pulled it up, then he lay back on his straw mattress and listened to the soft breathing of the other children in the hide.

Tumi was eight when he ran away from the conquerors. He

had seen two winters since then. His father had been a fisherman. He sold his fish in the market at Innswood; Tumi's mother
always sat at her husband's side and gutted the fish for their
wealthier customers. It was a good life — until the rebellion.
Tumi's father had always had a hot temper.

The people of Innswood chafed at the conquerors' laws, at
their greed and their cruelty. One cold, spring day, finding any
weapon they could, they banded together and refused to pay
their rents, refused to obey the laws that forbade them to hunt
in their own forests, to fish in their own streams. In less than an
hour, the conquerors, on their great horses, had cut down the
people of Innswood, until only the children were left. When the
children ran, the town was burned to the ground.

Tumi sat up. He rubbed his eyes. It wasn't safe for Sila and
Karli to travel alone. He must follow them, and quickly. Strapping
two spears to his back, he slung a bag over his shoulder. The bag
was always kept ready for flight, with rush-lights, dried berries,
and a roll of deerskin. Like the others, Tumi always slept fully
dressed.

He unwound the creeper, skimmed down it, and began to
run, hoping that he would soon find Sila and Karli. Even in the
dark, Tumi's feet kept to the track that he knew so well. He ran
swiftly, and was surprised not to come upon the others. He

dared not call out. Thorkil posted spies in the trees, ready to warn them if strangers appeared in the woods.

The track ended and Tumi hesitated. He was some distance from the tree-hides now. Perhaps he could risk a call. He could hear nothing but the rustling and snuffling of animals. Quickly, he withdrew a spear from its leather casing on his back. He held it steady at his side. "S-i-i-la!" he called. "Ka-ar-li!"

There was no reply. Which way should he go? Tumi looked at the sky and decided to keep moving forward, toward a cluster of stars that made the shape of a giant spoon. He had never learned the names of the stars, but he could recognize the patterns that they made.

A pale light began to filter through the trees. It was close to dawn. One by one, the stars faded into an ashen sky. Throughout the woods, birds woke up and filled the air with a multitude of songs. Still moving, Tumi tried to hear any sound that could tell him where Sila and Karli might have gone. Instead, he heard something that sent him scuttling into the undergrowth.

Hoofbeats. They were distant but coming closer every second. Soon they would be upon him. Tumi flattened himself under a thornbush and pulled his spear close, ready to use it if he had to. There was a chance that they would miss him, whoever they were, if he remained perfectly still until they passed. And then Tumi heard the howl. And he knew his moments of freedom were over. For only the conquerors hunted with dogs, and the dogs would surely find him.

So Tumi waited, clutching his spear. At least he could wound one of the loathsome tyrants, giving Sila and Karli a chance to get farther away. The horses were now only a few lengths down the track.

Tumi didn't hear the hound's stealthy approach until its bark of discovery erupted close to his ear. There was another bark, and another. The horses galloped up to him, and a harsh voice said, "Come out, whoever you are, before I throw this spear."

Tumi briefly closed his eyes. He knew it was hopeless. Two hounds were now eagerly sniffing at the thornbush. Suddenly, one of them thrust in its nose and nipped Tumi's ankle. The boy let out a yell and crawled onto the track.

"What have we here?" A rough voice chuckled.

"Just a kid," said the other man.

Still clutching his spear, Tumi got to his feet.

The first speaker had a face the color of a plum and was missing half an ear. The second man's skin was scarred by the pox and his lumpish nose was pricked like a worm-eaten apple.

The two horsemen wore chain mail beneath their orange-colored tunics, but their heads were bare. Their dun-colored hair had been roughly cut in a style the conquerors favored.

"So, who are you, boy? A thief? These are the king's woods now, and, by the look of that spear, such as it is" — Half-Ear gave another coarse chuckle — "you were doing some hunting."

Tumi couldn't stop himself. "Does the king own every hare in every wood?" he muttered softly.

At this, the two men threw back their heads and laughed.

"He's a bold one, Aelfric," said Worm-Apple.

"A rebel's son, no doubt," said Half-Ear, his eyes growing cold. "And, by the look of those breeches, he's stolen one of the king's seals."

"I found it," Tumi said defiantly. "It was washed ashore in a storm, and dead on the beach when I skinned it."

Worm-Apple leaned forward and brought his pockmarked face close to Tumi. "And had a nice little feast of it, eh?"

"No. The flesh was rotten." This was a lie. Tumi had shared the seal meat with the other tree children. The melted fat had kept their rush-lights burning for several months.

"You're a thief and a rebel," Half-Ear said gruffly. "But we'll let you go if you can tell us something."

"Yes?" Tumi was suspicious.

"We're looking for a boy on a camel." Half-Ear's blue eyes bored into Tumi's.

"A camel?" Tumi said slowly.

"A creature unknown in this land," said Worm-Apple. "But you can't mistake it." He wrinkled his pitted nose. "It's an ugly thing. It has a hump on its back and a very long neck. The boy has dark skin. . . ."

"And is, perhaps, accompanied by a wizard," said Half-Ear.

"Wizard?" Tumi repeated, his mind working furiously. These men were not friends. Tumi guessed that Sila and Karli would be traveling north, up the coast. He knew this was where Karli believed the camel would go — because of the sand.

"Don't look so gormless, boy," Worm-Apple shouted. "You know — a wizard. One of the ancient ones, a Briton. Eyes like a storm, hair like a thornbush, steel in his beard, robes like a bank of dead leaves."

"He's seen them," Half-Ear crowed triumphantly. "Haven't you, boy?"

Tumi could only nod.

"Where? Where did they go?" Half-Ear demanded.

Tumi pointed along the track behind the two horsemen.

Half-Ear frowned. "That way?"

"And then east, to the town, Innswood, where it stood before the fires." Tumi swung his arm at the sunrise.

"I hope you're telling the truth, boy," said Worm-Apple. "They're criminals, escaped from Castle Melyntha. We need to catch them before they can do any harm."

Tumi gave the man what he hoped was an innocent-looking stare.

"We'll have to get more men, Stenulf," said Half-Ear. "And I'll take this little rebel back to the castle. Three stableboys have taken sick. We could do with another."

Before Tumi could turn away, Half-Ear leaned down from the saddle and, seizing him under the arms, swung him up before him.

"Let me go! Traitors, bullies!" Tumi kicked at the man's shins. He twisted and squirmed, trying to free himself from the vicelike grip of Aelfric's strong arms. But it was useless. A half-starved boy stood no chance against a powerful, hardened soldier.

"You've got yourself a problem there, Aelfric," Stenulf chuckled. "Good luck to you."

Turning their horses, the two men galloped back down the track, passing beneath the tree-hides high in the branches. The thunder of hooves had already woken the children, and they watched Tumi's helpless struggles in dismay. They had just discovered that two more of their number were missing, and feared the worst.

Karli and Sila had turned their backs on the dawn light. They knew that they would find the sea in the west. They had not long left the track when they heard distant voices. A dog barked again and again, and there was an anguished scream. Sila pulled Karli to the ground. They lay still, hardly daring to breathe, and then crawled between the ivy covering the root of an old tree. Hidden behind the creepers, they listened for footsteps, for the snuffling of dogs, for hoofbeats.

The sun began to rise; its bright beams filtered through the trees and the woods rang with birdsong.

Karli sat up. "The conquerors came," he whispered, even though the danger seemed to have passed. "They caught someone, Sila."

The children looked into each other's faces, both of them knowing who had been caught.

"Tumi!" There was a catch in Sila's quiet voice. "It was my fault," she burst out. "I heard his voice. I should have known he would follow me."

"D'you think they . . ." Karli couldn't bring himself to ask the question.

"Killed him?" Sila shook her head. "Why should they? He's no danger to them. They've caught him, and now they'll make him their slave."

Karli frowned. His mouth trembled, but he held back the tears. "I hate them! I hate them!" he cried. "Nowhere is safe from them. Nowhere."

"There's always somewhere, Karli." Sila rubbed her eyes and smiled. "Come on, we're on our way to find a camel, remember?"

"And a king and a wizard," said Karli, jumping up.

It wasn't an easy journey. As the trees thinned, brambles and briars grew thicker. It took time to untangle themselves and tear their way through the undergrowth, even with their tough hide mittens. But, at last, they smelled the sea, they heard gulls crying overhead and, bursting out of the wood, found themselves on a stretch of soft sand dunes. Beyond the dunes lay the green-gray sea.

For a moment, they forgot everything and delighted in the feel of sand beneath their feet. They ran through the dunes and across the wet sand; flinging their bark clogs aside, they shrieked with breathless joy as they strode into the bubbling surf.

What pain! But what delicious relief to free their aching feet and soak them in the icy water. When they were almost numb with cold, they warmed themselves by jumping on the hard sand. Hunger drove them to the rock pools where they found handfuls of shrimp and small shellfish. They had no means of cooking them, but Tumi had taught them what they must avoid, and they had become accustomed to eating raw food, so their stomachs seldom objected. They slept in a warm hollow in the dunes. Sila spread her blanket of deerskins over them both and they closed their eyes, listening to the soft whispering of the marram grass.

In the morning, before they pulled on their clogs, they ran into the sea, just once more. A shoal of tiny fish washed over Karli's toes and he scooped up a handful and popped them in his mouth.

"What are you eating, Karli?" Sila ran up to him.

Karli pointed to the fish and Sila caught a handful for herself.

Their faces were bathed in sunlight as they walked across the beach. Sila had no idea where they were heading, or what would become of them. But she clung to the hope that they would find the little king. She was sure that, in his company, they would be safe.

Across the beach, up a bank of dunes, and then down to

another stretch of sand. They climbed a path to a cliff top where clusters of wild berries grew, and a tree of ripe nuts. They sat down and had a feast.

Afterward, they continued north, walking with the sun on the sides of their faces. The cliff sloped down eventually, into a vast bay. The sand was very pale, making it look like a field of snow. The sea had retreated so far that it was no more than a thin blue line on the horizon, and the cliffs that surrounded the bay were almost as distant.

Sila judged that it would take half the night to walk around the bay, whereas, if they ran across the sand, they would reach the headland on the other side before the sun went down.

"If you're right, Karli," she said, "and the camel likes sand, then he would have crossed here, and at this very moment might be resting on the other side."

"Let's go!" Karli ran onto the sand while Sila followed at a slower pace. She had a sudden moment of uncertainty; the cliffs were so very far away. Banishing her doubt, she ran onto the beach.

They were halfway across when they heard the roar. At first they couldn't make out what it was, and then Sila realized that it was the roar of water. The tide was coming in, faster than she could ever have imagined. In a few seconds it was lapping at their feet. Sila grabbed Karli's hand and turned toward the shore. "Run!" she cried.

Karli didn't move. "I can't," he screamed. His feet were sinking into the sand. It was swallowing him.

Sila put her hands beneath his arms and pulled with all her might. With a dreadful sucking sound, Karli tugged one foot free, and then the other. They staggered toward the distant shore, while the tide rushed after them. Soon, it was gurgling around their knees.

"Faster, Karli!" Sila begged. "Faster." She looked at the shore and her eyes widened in horror. The sea had gotten there first. Waves, higher than her head, were rising, rolling, and roaring. The water had played a cruel trick. It had surrounded them, and now her own feet were sinking into the deadly sand.

Tumi had told them stories of drowned fishermen. Soon she would know what it was like to drown. Hugging Karli tight, she closed her eyes.

"We're going to drown, Sila, aren't we?" Karli sobbed. "I wish Tumi had taught us to swim."

CHAPTER 8
Eri's Dream

A howling wind now accompanied the waves that rushed to the shore. The clamor of air and water battered Sila's mind. She couldn't feel her feet; she was numb with cold. Karli was shivering violently and Sila realized that she, too, was shaking uncontrollably.

"P-p-perhaps we sh-sh-shall fr-fr-freeze to death," Karli's teeth chattered in his head, but he had stopped crying.

It was almost dark.

Sila thought she heard a voice in the wind. She looked up and saw a great bird hovering above them. Its wings were a dusky red against the night sky.

"Girl," called the voice. "Lift up your arms."

So this is what happens when you die, thought Sila. *A giant bird carries you into the heavens.*

"Girl! Do as I say!" The bird came nearer. It flew around them. And now Sila could see that it had a human face, a dark face with a hint of gold in its black hair.

"You came!" Karli's voice shook with cold, yet he didn't sound surprised to see the strange boy, treading air.

"You won't drown, I promise you!" A smile lit the dark face, and the boy landed in the water before them. Sila was surprised by the loud splash he made. She hadn't expected him to make sounds like other mortals.

"I c-can't move. The s-sand is sw-swallowing me." She forced the words through her chattering teeth.

The boy pulled off his cloak and swung it around Sila's shoulders. Its folds enveloped Karli, still clinging to her waist.

"My name is Timoken," said the boy, fastening the cloak with a silver pin.

"I'm Sila." A glow like the sun's warmth was spreading through her body. She could feel her feet again, and pulled each one up with all the strength she had left. Her toes wriggled. Her ankles came free. "I'm almost out," she cried, her shivers subsiding. She tugged again, and felt one foot slip out of the sand's grip, and then the other. "Yes!" she sang.

"Good," said Timoken. "Now, put your arms around my waist, and believe that you can fly."

"I can fly?" Sila found that she believed what she said, because she had to; there was no other way to survive.

"And I can fly, too!" The water was up to Karli's chest, but he gazed at Timoken with an eager smile.

"Hold Sila as tight as you can, and believe," said Timoken. "Now we'll fly!"

The current was beginning to drag them backward. It was all Sila could do to stand upright. She clung to Timoken's waist as he swung his arms up and out into the air.

The two children weighed almost nothing compared to Gabar. Timoken lifted them into the sky with ease, and then sailed into the moaning wind. Below them, the rising water swelled and splashed, and Sila and Karli could feel the wind from the waves brushing their bare feet. The red cloak billowed around them like a sail.

All light had left the sky when Timoken landed on the headland. Sila released her grip and fell to the ground with Karli still clinging to her.

"You're safe now." Timoken tapped Karli's shoulder.

Karli let go of Sila and sat up. "You saved us, sir," he said.

Timoken grinned. "Not sir. Call me Timoken. And it was my camel that saved you. He saw you and came to tell me."

"My name is Karli, and once I lived in a house and had a family." He turned to Sila. "And she did, too."

"Then we are all in the same boat," said Timoken, smiling. He put more brushwood on the fire, and in its sudden blaze he saw the girl's face. She might have been ninety years old, with her hollow cheeks and the dark rings beneath her eyes, and yet she had a lively, inquisitive expression.

"The first time we saw you, you were talking to your camel," Sila said, almost accusingly.

"Yes." Timoken nodded. "I often do."

"I see. And you can fly, and so can he." She pointed at Gabar. "What else can you do? And where are you from?"

"Africa," Timoken yawned, "and I get tired, just like you do. I propose to give you some food, and then go to sleep. Are you agreeable?"

"I'm very hungry," said Karli. Sila smiled.

They shared some berries and dried meat, and drank from the water bag that Timoken had filled at the stream. Karli's eyes were already closing when Timoken lay beside him and pulled the moon cloak over the three of them.

"Why is it so warm?" Sila asked sleepily. "Your cloak?"

"Because you need it to be," Timoken replied.

Sila thought about this and fell asleep knowing that she wouldn't get a better answer just yet.

They slept deeply, all three exhausted by the day's events. Before Timoken opened his eyes the next morning, he was aware of the figure beside him. He sat up. The sun was rising and the grasses on the headland danced with light. The wizard stood looking down at him.

"Eri!" Timoken said joyfully.

The wizard didn't return his greeting. He stared down at the boy, his black eyebrows drawn together in a scowl. Ignoring the children beside Timoken, Eri grunted, "You lied to me, boy."

"I don't lie!" Timoken sprang to his feet.

"Then you didn't tell me the truth."

"When?" Timoken asked wildly.

"When you told me the story of your life." Eri's voice dropped a register and he ground his teeth as though he were chewing on bones.

"There's nothing of importance that I haven't told you, unless it's a brief thing, a meal I took, a place I saw, a coin I multiplied. I don't know. My life has been so *long*."

Sila and Karli had woken up. They sat huddled together beneath the cloak, staring at the wizard in dismay. Even the camel got to his feet, spitting and snorting with anxiety.

"Ahhh!" groaned Eri. He thumped the ground with a staff he had recently acquired: a slim branch that he had stripped of its bark. It tapered at the top into a spike.

"Eri, what have you learned?" begged Timoken. "It must be something — *dreadful*."

The wizard strode away from him, turned, and marched back. "You didn't tell me about the ring." He prodded Timoken's chest with the tip of his staff.

"My sister's ring?" Timoken was mystified. "I did. I did tell you."

"You did not speak of its character, and that it's in THERE." Eri jabbed the moon cloak with his staff. The two children leaped out, dropping the cloak and scuttling behind the camel.

Timoken looked at the cloak. He picked it up and clasped it to him. "My cloak was made by the last forest-jinni. I can see him in my sister's ring. And I know that a part of his spirit lives in this cloak. It is a good thing, Eri. It has saved lives."

"Ach!" Again Eri thumped the earth with his staff. "It attracts danger. You must get rid of it." Reaching into a sack that hung from his belt, the wizard pulled out a dead hare and flung it at the boy's feet. "Cook my breakfast and I'll tell you why."

Timoken looked vacantly at the hare. Held close to his heart, the moon cloak calmed his racing pulse. He was angry with Eri, and afraid of him.

While Timoken stood motionless, Sila crept from behind the camel and picked up the hare. "I'll skin it," she said, looking fearlessly at the wizard.

Eri scowled. "Who are you?"

"I'm Sila." She glanced back at Karli, two paces behind her. "And that's Karli."

"Rebels' children," said the wizard.

"Innswood was our home," Sila agreed. "Then we were forest people, and now we belong to Timoken, because he saved our lives," she hesitated, and added daringly, "with his cloak."

"Skin the hare, child," Eri said a little more kindly. "You look starved. Boy" — he pointed at Karli — "build up the fire."

Timoken watched Karli busying about under the trees; he watched Sila take a sharp flint from her wet bag and begin to skin the hare. He felt dizzy with apprehension. His sword, his shield, and his knife had all been left behind at the castle, but he still had his cloak. The best of all his possessions. He would never let it go.

"Come and share our breakfast," the wizard said gruffly. "I won't take the cloak from you, but you must know the truth of it."

Karli's fire burned brightly, and the smell of cooked meat filled the small copse of trees. Cautiously, Timoken approached and took a place between the children. Eri stared at him from the other side of the fire. Timoken looked away from the wizard's compelling gaze. There was wickedness in Eri. There had to be, for him to say such things about the moon cloak.

They chewed in silence for a while, and when the wizard spoke again, his voice took on the sound of the crackling fire and the soft pattering of leafless twigs.

"My dreams are not always comforting," Eri began. "Sometimes they make no sense. They are a half-and-half sort of thing."

"So that's why you went away," Timoken muttered. "To dream."

"I have to be alone," said Eri, frowning at the interruption. "You asked me to tell you about your sister, and your friends, and also about a certain — girl."

Timoken nodded. He felt Sila's eyes on him, and he blushed.

"And so I dreamed," the wizard went on. "I saw a grave of stones, and Britons, like me, praying beside it. False prayers, for the grave was empty. I saw painted shields: an eagle, a wolf, and a bear. And I saw your sister hand in hand with a tiny child. And I wondered if it was mine."

"Yours?" Timoken exclaimed. "But . . ."

"You think I didn't have a wife, boy?" growled Eri. "You think I didn't have a son who had a wife? You think I didn't have a grandchild? I had all these, but someone came to my dwelling and took them. They were found, later, all dead. But my grand-child was gone."

The silence that followed this pronouncement was so profound even Gabar dropped his head in concern.

After a moment, Timoken said, "I am so sorry, Eri. I didn't guess."

"No," Eri mumbled. "It's not your fault."

They began to eat again, a little uncomfortably, before Timoken asked awkwardly, "Did you dream of HER, Eri? Of Berenice?"

"I did," said Eri. "I saw her in the Widows' Tower. She is sewing with other ladies, all in a circle. There is a tap at the window. No one hears but her. And when she looks, there is a hare at the window, very high, as if it has flown there." Eri shrugged and looked at Timoken. "So now you have it. And good luck if you can make sense of it."

"Thank you." Timoken tried not to frown, and he tried to keep the image of Berenice and the hare clear in his head, but Eri was still talking and dragging Timoken's thoughts away from the girl and the hare.

"You told me that your cloak was made of a spider's web, that much is true," said Eri, "but when I dreamed of your cloak, I saw a sheet of silver, sparkling with a thousand colors. I saw a being, small with dark wings, splashing the web with water from a pool. It was fed by tears that spilled from the eyes of creatures that knelt beside it. Beautiful creatures: their eyes were large and golden, their ears soft and pointed, their tails ringed in blues and purples. I knew we should never see their like again."

Timoken heard a quiet sniff and glanced at Sila. She rubbed her eyes and smiled at him.

"And then I saw the winged being run across the forest floor," Eri went on. "It held the web like a banner floating behind it, brushing the dewy petals of flowers that would never bloom again. While it ran, the winged being sang a spell, and that was the worst of it, Timoken."

Timoken shrank under the fierce gray eyes. "Why?" he whispered.

"It had a slight, sweet voice," said Eri. "Very beguiling. It said that a newborn child wrapped in the web would live forever, would be a marvelous magician and" — the wizard stared at Timoken — "AND would have only one foot in the real world. The other would remain in the realm of enchantments. What have you to say about that, Timoken, eh? You were that newborn child."

Timoken clutched the web even tighter. "What's so wrong?" he said.

"Aaah!" Eri stamped his foot. "It means they'll be after you, and us. They'll follow their noses, sniff out the web — and you. Because you're still a part of their world."

"Who?" asked Sila.

"Beings from the realm of enchantments, girl," the wizard answered gruffly.

"Surely some are friendly," Sila said boldly.

Eri spat on the grass. "Silly girl. It's the greedy ones we have to fear. The demons. They'll want that cloak, and they'll kill to get it. They're here already. Did you know that?" The wizard scowled. "I heard them, felt them, down in the forest. I had to make this wand to protect myself."

"I'm more scared of the conquerors," said Karli. "Could I have a wand, too?"

Eri turned and walked away from them, muttering under his breath. Timoken watched the wizard marching through the bracken. He swung his staff over his head, as though warding off a swarm of invisible bees.

"Are you afraid of the wizard?" Karli asked Timoken.

"A little," Timoken admitted.

"Shall we build a house here," asked Sila, "to keep us safe?"

Timoken grinned. "No. We shall build a castle, down there in the forest."

Sila's ringed eyes grew round with amazement. "In spite of the demons?"

"We shall—" He was interrupted by a loud cry overhead. Looking up, he saw a flying creature, its vast wings spread against the light. It cried again, a low, melancholy sound, ending in a cough. And then it was falling, rather too fast, toward them.

It landed with a *crackle* and a *bang*, right on top of the fire. Karli screamed and Gabar let out a powerful snort of alarm. Sila and Timoken stared at the newcomer, too surprised to utter a sound.

CHAPTER 9
A Dragon

The creature was the size of a large hound, a very overfed and heavy hound. Its belly was so big, it covered the fire entirely, smothering the flames.

In all his travels, Timoken had never seen anything like this beast. It was covered in rounded, pewter-colored scales, and the wings sprouting from its shoulders were like those of a large bat. A line of diamond-shaped platelets ran from the top of its head, along its spine, and down to the very tip of its long, thick tail. In some respects, its snout resembled a hound's, too, but if Timoken was not mistaken, a wreath of smoke curled gently from each of its nostrils.

The creature turned its long neck and looked around at its audience with bewildered golden eyes. It drew back its lips in what looked like a hopeful smile. Timoken stepped away from it. Those sharp teeth gave its smile a dangerous edge. It turned its gaze on the camel, who snorted, "What is it, Family?"

"What is it?" asked Sila and Karli in whispers.

Timoken shrugged. "What are you?" he ventured, giving the creature a tentative grin. He didn't yet know its language.

It seemed delighted to be spoken to, however, and, standing on its hind legs, rushed up to Timoken, waving its tail.

"Whoa!" cried Timoken, putting up his hand.

Gabar gave a protective bellow and the creature stopped in its tracks. It let out a husky sort of whine, giving Timoken a sense of its language.

"What are you?" he asked in a similar whining voice.

"Master knows," it said.

Timoken frowned. Where was its master? Again, he asked, "What are you?"

The strange creature seemed disappointed. It dropped onto its forelegs and gazed wistfully at Timoken. He noticed the scaly feet planted squarely in front of the creature's round body. Each toe ended in a long, sharp claw.

"What shall we do with it?" asked Sila.

Its head swiveled in her direction and she took a step back.

"I think we should feed it," said Karli. "In case it's hungry, and . . ." He rolled his eyes and grimaced.

Timoken scratched his head. "We can't do anything with it," he said. "We'll just have to wait for it to make up its mind."

"About what?" asked Sila.

"Whether it wants to stay or go."

Karli stepped a little closer to the creature. "If we go, d'you think it'll follow?"

"Let's see." Timoken swung around and walked to the edge of the trees. He had only taken a few steps when he heard the heavy creature thumping behind him.

"It's following," said Sila.

Timoken stopped. He smiled to himself. "It wants to be family."

"Family!" Sila said doubtfully.

But the creature didn't wait behind Timoken. It ran straight past him, its thick tail sweeping aside the bracken.

A voice carried through the air. "There you are!" Eri came striding up the hill, and with joyful squeals, the creature ran into the wizard's outstretched arms. He hugged it fiercely, until all that could be seen of the creature was its spiky head, peeping through the folds of the wizard's tattered robe.

After a lot of tender murmuring from the wizard, and grunts of pleasure from the creature, Eri looked up at the three children gathered at the edge of the trees.

"You've met her, then?" called the wizard, his bad temper apparently forgotten.

"Her?" said Timoken.

"My friend Enid." The wizard ambled toward them with his friend bouncing beside him.

"I hope you don't think I'm ignorant, Eri," said Timoken when the wizard reached them, "but what is she?" He glanced at the creature that was now happily sniffing the old man's shoes.

"What d'you think she is?" said Eri indignantly.

"I don't know," Timoken admitted irritably.

"I think I do," said Karli. "I've seen her face, or something like it, on the church at Innswood, before it was burned down, of course."

"No," Sila told him. "That was a carving of something mythical."

Timoken thought he had seen so much more of the world than Karli and Sila. How was it that he had never seen a creature like Enid?

"Enid is no myth, girl." Eri gave a gleeful chuckle. "But I have to keep her secret, or she would be killed for sport. She hides herself so well these days, sometimes I cannot find her for a whole season. This time I thought I'd lost her forever." He ran his fingers down Enid's scaly neck. "But now that you've seen her, there's no need for secrecy."

"And she can stay with us forever," said Karli, clapping his hands. Then, suddenly serious, he asked, "She doesn't eat people, does she?"

The wizard's thin lips framed a slanting sort of smile. "She won't eat you, now that she knows you," he said. "But I can't guarantee that she won't eat *anyone*."

"So what *is* she?" begged Timoken.

The wizard stared at him in disbelief. "For goodness' sake, boy. Are you so ignorant? Enid is a dragon."

"A *dragon*!" Timoken's mouth fell open. "I've heard of dragons, of course. I have seen their likenesses on churches in France and Spain, but they were very different from Enid."

"She's overweight," Eri admitted. "When she's lonely, she eats a great deal and does very little exercise."

"So what does she eat mostly?" asked Karli.

"Fish," Eri replied. "She's a great swimmer, when she can be bothered, and birds. She's very fond of seagulls." He glanced at the children and added, "It's the salt, you see. She loves salt."

None of them had noticed the approach of dark clouds, and

they were taken by surprise when heavy raindrops began to beat down on their heads.

"Into the forest," said the wizard. "We'll keep dry there."

Had Eri forgotten the forest demons? Timoken wondered. Or did the dragon make him feel safer?

They trooped across the field of bracken, Eri taking long strides while Enid leaped beside him. Sila and Karli bounded over the bracken behind him. Timoken and Gabar brought up the rear. The camel hated rain, but he didn't seem to be in a hurry to get out of it.

Lowering his big head close to Timoken's ear, Gabar confided, "I don't like the look of those claws."

Timoken knew what his camel meant. "I'm sure the wizard wouldn't let his dragon do anything dangerous," he said quietly.

"Or those teeth," added Gabar, ignoring Timoken's reassurance.

"We'll be safe," said Timoken, patting his camel's neck.

When they reached the forest, they followed Eri to a huge oak tree, still in leaf. Its great branches were wide enough to cover them all, and as the rain pattered harmlessly all about him, Timoken couldn't believe there was any evil in the forest. He felt as safe and untroubled as he had all those years ago, in his secret

African kingdom. He had no doubts at all that this ancient forest was the place for him to make a home. If only his sister were here, his sister and the five loyal companions who had traveled with him through so many dangers.

One thought led to another, and soon Timoken was wondering about the wizard's mysterious dream. The signs he had seen, and the hare at the high window. What could it all mean?

"The rain has stopped." Eri's voice cut through Timoken's thoughts. "It's time for work."

Sila and Karli knew what to do. They were already running to collect bracken and dead grass from the field.

"We need a shelter." The wizard gave Timoken a sly look. "No doubt you have ways of finding timber for a frame."

"I do," Timoken agreed. He was about to walk farther into the forest when the dragon suddenly shook out her wings.

Gabar gave an anxious bellow and stamped the ground.

"I'll take my camel," said Timoken, glancing at the dragon.

"She won't hurt him," chuckled Eri. "She's off to do some fishing."

No sooner had he said this than Enid rose up through the trees, surprisingly fast for a fat dragon, and into the sky.

"I need Gabar to carry the timber," said Timoken, glad of an excuse to keep his camel close.

"Naturally." Eri grinned. "See that you return before the light begins to fail."

"I will." Timoken grunted to his camel and they set off into the forest. They hadn't gone far when Gabar began to grumble, as Timoken knew he would.

"Trees! Trees! Trees!" snorted the camel. "Why do we always have to make our home beneath the trees? Why can't we live beside the sand?"

Timoken sighed. "Here we are hidden. Out on the coast, people would see us."

"There are no people," argued the camel.

"I'm sure there will be," said Timoken. "The conquerors don't like prisoners escaping, especially if one of them is a wizard. As for me, well, I might have killed someone, Gabar."

To the camel, this didn't sound very serious. Men were always killing one another, so were animals. "I have stepped on a lizard," he muttered, "more than once, for all I know. But no one put me in prison for it."

Timoken laughed so loudly a flock of jackdaws rose from the treetops and whirled away in a chattering cloud.

"Gabar, you are very wise," said Timoken. "I'm so glad that you are my family."

They wandered farther into the trees, but now Gabar would

continually stop to chew the undergrowth, and Timoken was so afraid of losing him that he reluctantly slowed down. But he was impatient to find a fallen branch, a good straight one, that he could multiply.

Gabar was drinking from a stream when Timoken saw the branch he wanted. It was bobbing gently in the water, on the other side of the stream. Timoken took off his boots and paddled across. He pulled the branch up onto the bank and sat there, preparing himself. Multiplying shells and coins and hare's skins was a fairly simple task, but branches were bigger and heavier. First, he must get it into shape.

Timoken ran his hands along the bark. His fingers touched the dead twigs sprouting from the wood, the rough knobs, and patches of fungi. After a while, a smooth post began to emerge from the branch; it was as long as Eri and as wide as one of Timoken's legs. He sat back, pleased with himself, and began to chant in the language of his homeland.

The camel looked up and watched as a long post took shape beside the first. Then came another, and another.

Timoken found that his cloak was getting in the way. He took it off and hung it on a low branch. Soon he had six identical posts. How many would the wizard want? he wondered. He started to make another.

A thin mist began to drift through the trees. Gabar heard something, or rather, he sensed it. He crossed the stream and stood behind Timoken. "Family, there is something here," he grunted. "Not good."

Timoken noticed nothing. He was too intent on his work.

All at once, the camel bellowed and stamped the earth. Timoken stopped chanting. He jumped up, and was just in time to see his cloak disappearing into the shadows.

"No-o-o-o-o!" cried Timoken, giving chase.

"I told you! I told you!" the camel bleated, as he crashed through the undergrowth after Timoken.

"Who took it?" yelled Timoken. "Who took my cloak?"

"*They* did," snorted the camel. "I told you it was *them*."

"Who? Who?"

"Things. Pale things." Gabar didn't know how else to describe the things he saw.

Timoken ran on, blindly leaping fallen trees, tumbling through thickets and briars, until he stopped, breathless and aching. The cloak had vanished utterly. He didn't know which way to go. He sat on a moss-covered rock and shouted his fury, kicking the ground in frustration.

A moment later Sila and Karli appeared, followed by the wizard.

"What's all this noise?" grumbled Eri. "You'll wake the spirits with that racket."

"My cloak has gone," Timoken said miserably.

"Ah," the wizard sighed. "I can't say I'm surprised."

There was a sudden deep roar, then another, and another.

"Are there monsters in this forest?" Karli asked, his eyes searching the shadows.

"Without a doubt," said Eri.

CHAPTER 10
Outnumbered by Animals

Timoken recognized those savage roars. Without a word he was off, bounding through the forest like a wild deer. His heart leaped, his spirits soared.

"Sun Cat! Flame Chin! Star!" he cried.

Sila grabbed Eri's sleeve. "Has Timoken gone mad?"

Eri patted her hand. "I think not."

"He'll be eaten," Karli said fearfully.

"Unlikely," said Eri. "Let's find out."

They followed the sound of Timoken's voice, stepping over dry twigs and rustling scrub as cautiously and quietly as they could.

Timoken had already reached the source of those deep roars. In a sunlit clearing, three leopards stood shoulder to shoulder, their coats dappled by shadows. They varied in color from dark copper to pale yellow; one had a hint of orange beneath his chin. Timoken's red cloak was spread at their feet.

"Sun Cat!" Timoken stroked the head of the copper-colored leopard. "Flame Chin!" He fondled the ears of the leopard with a splash like a flame beneath his chin.

When he came to the third and palest leopard, Timoken wrapped his arms around his neck and murmured, "Star!"

There was a gasp behind him and he turned to see Eri and the two children peering at him through the thin stems of a hazel bush.

"They saved it!" Timoken lifted his cloak and fixed it around his shoulders. "Whoever stole it won't try again."

His three friends didn't move, didn't utter a sound.

"I'm sorry, I didn't introduce you," Timoken said with a reassuring grin. "Sun Cat, Flame Chin, and Star." He pointed at the leopards in turn.

But still his friends didn't move or speak.

The group behind the hazel bush remained where they were while the leopards surrounded Timoken, rubbing their heads against his body and filling the glade with purrs as loud as drumbeats.

It was Karli who stepped out first. "Are they lions?" he said, almost in a whisper.

"No, they're leopards," said Timoken. He turned to the three big cats. "Friend," he grunted, taking Karli's hand.

"Friend," growled the leopards.

Karli gave a little start.

"They won't hurt you," Timoken assured him. "I've told them you're a friend."

Tentatively, Karli touched Sun Cat's head. He was rewarded with a purr.

Eri stepped around the hazel, followed by Sila.

"Friends!" Timoken told the leopards.

"Friends!" they grunted.

"Are you speaking their language, Timoken?" The wizard frowned, partly in disbelief, partly in disapproval.

"Yes," Timoken admitted. "I'm sorry, Eri. I said that I'd told you everything about my past, but, somehow, I forgot the leopards because —"

"Why?" asked Eri sternly.

"Because . . . because their lives are secret, even from me. That's the nature of leopards."

"But these are no ordinary leopards," said Eri.

"No." Timoken hesitated. "I think I'd better tell you about them."

"I think you had." Eri settled himself on the ground, while Sila and Karli knelt on either side of him. Timoken sat cross-legged before them. The leopards paced about the clearing, sniffing the air where the shadows were darkest and growling softly to one another.

Timoken told his friends about the viridees of the African forest. He told how one of them had killed a leopard and let hyenas feed on her prey, a dead gazelle. He told how he had found three leopard cubs, now motherless because of the viridee, and how he, Timoken, had killed the viridee and driven off the hyenas. "I took the carcass back to the cubs and fed them," said Timoken, remembering it all as if it were yesterday, "and then I wrapped them in the web of the last moon spider."

"Did the web cast a spell on them?" asked Sila, with a catch in her throat.

Timoken nodded. "And their lives were in my hands for a while. But they grew very fast and soon became my guardians. They've saved me from many dangerous situations."

"Did they swim over the sea?" Karli's eyes were huge with wonder.

"No, they hid themselves on a ship, while Gabar and I flew above it."

Sun Cat suddenly let out a deeper growl. He was standing behind the wizard, who nervously hunched his shoulders. Beyond the leopard, Timoken could make out the dim outlines of a camel and a dragon.

"Gabar! Enid! Come closer," called Timoken. "It's quite safe."

Gabar and Enid stayed where they were.

"Can you blame them?" said Eri.

Gabar knew the leopards well, but he preferred to keep his distance. He would rather Enid kept her distance from him, too, but she seemed to have taken a liking to him. For her part, Enid was very suspicious of the three large, growling, spotted cats. She decided to stick close to the camel.

Sila giggled. "We are outnumbered by animals," she said.

Eri began to chuckle, and Karli and Timoken laughed as well.

The animals appeared to be offended. At least they had that in common.

Eri looked around the clearing. He gazed at the wide oaks that encircled them and listened to the splash and gurgle of a small stream that ran nearby. "Here!" the wizard declared. "We will make our shelter here."

The animals watched them set to work. Eri instructed. Sila and Karli fetched and carried. Timoken multiplied posts, setting them in the ground and lacing them with cords of dry grass and ivy. And as he worked, he thought of the castle he would build: strong, tall, and impregnable.

"Your mind's not on your work," Eri complained, picking up a fallen post. He clicked his tongue and walked around the small dwelling that was taking shape, tapping the wood and rethreading the ivy. "We need rushes," he said, pointing at the roof, "and more grass, long grass, to bind the stems. Karli and Sila, off to the field with you; Timoken, to the stream."

They stopped, briefly, to eat the fish that Enid had brought, and then they worked on into the night. The moon was rising when Eri at last declared that nothing more could be done just yet. The shelter was almost weatherproof and his bones told him that the rain would hold off for a while. They crawled into the shelter and immediately fell asleep on beds of leaves and bracken.

Timoken woke several hours later. Not a scrap of light penetrated the thick walls of bracken and ivy, but a slice of moonlight could be seen where the rough edge of the door met the wooden frame.

Outside, leaves rustled, and Timoken sensed, rather than heard, the slight movement of animals. A sudden, distant wail quickened his heartbeat and then he remembered the leopards and smiled to himself.

There was a second wail, a high melancholy sound. On the other side of the shelter, Sila sat up. Timoken could see her pale, worn face and her large gray eyes staring at the door in terror.

"It's all right, Sila," Timoken whispered. "The leopards are close."

She looked at him, the terror still plain on her thin face. "Wolves," she said huskily.

"If it is a wolf, it won't get past the leopards," he said. "And anyway, I can—" He stopped himself from saying any more.

"You can speak with wolves, too, I suppose," she said, unsmiling.

"If necessary," he muttered.

The next wail, when it came, was much closer. It was not wolflike in the least. Beside Timoken, the wizard grumbled in his sleep. Beyond the wizard, Karli sat bolt upright and gave a little cry.

Sila leaned over and took his hand. "You're safe, Karli," she told him. "Timoken's leopards are outside."

"I can't hear them." Karli looked at Timoken. "Will they chase the wolves away? Will they kill them?"

Before Timoken could answer, another sound came from outside, very close to the leafy wall: a leopard growl. There was a tremendous commotion in the undergrowth: a snapping, brushing, thumping, growling, and shrieking. Gabar bellowed. Enid screeched, and then, all at once, a profound silence fell upon the forest.

"Gone," said Eri, without raising his head. "Now, perhaps, we can get some sleep."

So Eri had been awake all the time.

"He just didn't want to wake up too much," Sila remarked, "and have to talk to us."

"But what has gone?" asked Karli.

"The wolves, of course," said Sila in a comfortable tone.

Timoken didn't contradict her. Those melancholy wails didn't come from a wolf. No, that was different.

"I wish we still lived in the trees," Karli mumbled as he curled himself into his bed of leaves.

"But not with Thorkil," Sila said softly.

Timoken knew that he wouldn't sleep until he had looked outside. He got up and went to the door. A rough circle of ivy hooked the door to a notch on the frame. Timoken lifted the ivy and pushed the door open. He stepped out and felt his way around the shelter.

The camel crouched beneath a tree, his heavy head lowered in sleep. Enid rested in his shadow; her eyes were closed and gentle wreaths of smoke curled from her snout as she breathed.

Timoken squinted into the darkness beyond them. And there they were. The leopards stood erect, ears pricked, their coats glowing like embers.

"Sleep, king," said Sun Cat.

"All is well," added Flame Chin.

"And the wailing creatures?" asked Timoken.

Three pairs of gold eyes stared back at him.

"We can manage them," said Star.

"But what are they?"

The leopards shifted their paws, they inclined their heads, one to another, as if conferring. At last they spoke. "Creatures of rot, of must and mist, of cold."

Timoken shivered. "Must and mist," he said to himself. Bidding the leopards good night, he went back to bed. As he pulled his cloak over himself, the faint, silvery outlines of a web appeared in the red velvet. Caught in the web's heart was the face of the forest-jinni; his huge saffron-colored eyes stared up at Timoken, his long nose partly hid his thin, drooping mouth, and his hairless brow was wrinkled with concern.

"Have the viridees followed me from Africa?" Timoken whispered to the face.

"Not them." The jinni's voice was hardly more than a breath. "Little king, because of me, you will always be part of both the world of men and the realm of enchantments. Some of them wicked. They exist in every corner of the world."

"Will I never escape this — condition?"

"Never," breathed the jinni. "Forgive?"

"How can I do otherwise?"

The threadlike corners of the jinni's mouth drew themselves into a smile. "But you will have many, many rewards. And what is a reward without a sacrifice?"

Timoken looked at his sleeping friends, he gazed up at the mossy roof of his new home, and he thought of the grand castle that he would soon begin to build. A castle for his friends, for his sister, and for Beri, without whom his castle could never be a home. One day soon, he must return to Castle Melyntha and rescue them. It wouldn't be an easy venture, for the guards were ever-watchful, but it was not impossible. "Yes," he said to himself, "there will be many, many rewards."

CHAPTER 11
The Enchanted Wall

Sila and Karli were barely awake when Timoken left the shelter next morning. Eri was already at work; a mysterious humming could be heard somewhere close. It was accompanied by Enid's busy little snorts.

Naturally, the leopards were nowhere to be seen, but Gabar was munching leaves beside the shelter. Timoken patted his neck and said, "Stay close to the children while I'm away."

"Where are you going?" grunted the camel.

"To my castle."

Timoken recognized the look of doubt and disapproval on the camel's face.

"You don't have a castle," Gabar snorted.

"Not yet," said Timoken. "But you wait!" He took a leap across the clearing and began to rise into the air.

At that moment, Karli looked out of the shelter and saw a figure in the morning sky. "Timoken," he cried. "Don't go!"

"I'll be back," called Timoken. He turned in the air, as though he were swimming, and disappeared above the treetops.

Now that he was alone, Timoken's conscience began to prickle. It was so good to be high above the earth, away from the toil and danger of the world below. *Soon, when my castle is built,* he told himself, *there will be shelter and safety for a hundred people.*

The countryside beneath was beautiful. Timoken flew over forests, hills, rivers, and clearings. Fields began to appear, marked by low stone walls. Some were tilled, showing dark red earth. And then, all at once, he was above a town set in a wide valley.

Two buildings dominated the town. At one end, on top of a steep hill, there was a castle. It was the same dark red as the earth of the fields. At the other end, set apart from the town, there was an abbey. It was red, like the castle, and wonderfully decorated with carved stone flowers and creatures.

"Yes!" Timoken clapped his hands and turned a somersault in the air. "My castle shall be red."

He flew above the castle, and looked down on a courtyard bristling with activity. There were armed soldiers everywhere, even on the roof. In a field below the castle, three great warhorses cropped the grass, while a herd of pigs rooted in the muddy pen beside them.

Tonight, thought Timoken. As he hovered in the air, a group of soldiers suddenly looked up; one pointed at him. He spread his arms, hoping his cloak would look like the wings of a bird. As he flew off, he heard an arrow whisper through the air behind him. He soared upward, his arms raised, his hands together, fingers pointed like a dart. Soon he was beyond the sight of almost any living thing on Earth. Only the birds could see him.

When Timoken got back to the shelter, no one was there but Gabar.

"Where are the others?" Timoken asked.

"Listen," said the camel.

Faint laughter could be heard, then the snatch of a tune, far away in the trees. Timoken followed the sound. He found Sila and Karli building a low wall of oak leaves.

"We're building a magic wall," Karli told him.

"A wall?" Timoken wasn't impressed. "That's not a wall."

"An enchanted wall," said Sila, "to keep out the demons."

"Built of leaves?" Timoken touched them with the toe of his boot.

"Don't!" Sila scolded, pulling him back. "Eri's power comes

from the earth; his magic is old, older than the forest. It's just as strong as yours."

"And it's not only leaves," Karli added. "See, there's yellow gorse and dried meadowsweet."

"I'm sorry." Timoken could sense it now, the bond between the leaves and the floor of this ancient forest. He put out his hand and felt a swirl of air above the wall. It was neither hot nor cold, but so potent it seeped between his fingers, spreading them wide.

"See!" Karli grinned at him.

Timoken withdrew his hand. "Yes. I can feel it."

The wizard's voice came rattling through the trees. "Where have you been, boy? We needed you here."

Brandishing his staff, Eri strode up to Timoken. "Well, have you brought food? Have you brought herbs for my wall? In the name of all the gods, where have you been?"

Timoken felt like a guilty child, even though he was older, by far, than the wizard. "I've been exploring," he said sheepishly.

"What did you find?" Eri thumped his staff and Enid came pounding to his side.

"I found a town," said Timoken, avoiding the wizard's fierce gray eyes. "It was many, many lengths from here, but we could reach it if we needed to."

"We don't need to," Eri said grimly. "Conquerors will be there, soldiers, busybodies, spies on the lookout for strangers."

Timoken kicked the ground lightly. "What can I do for you, then?"

"Bring gorse and meadowsweet. Sila has found a pile of sharp flints. Take one and cut some willow stems. There's a tree by the stream. Make a basket from the stems and fill the basket with oak leaves. Our wall has a long way to go."

Timoken hesitated, but he had to ask. "What's it for, Eri? The wall?"

The wizard glared at him in amazement. "What d'you think it's for? To protect us."

"But here, in the forest? The leopards can protect us."

Sila and Karli followed the argument with troubled eyes. They didn't dare to interrupt, and only wanted the friction to end.

The wizard's eyebrows were drawn together in a thunderous line. "Have you learned nothing, African? We are at war with everything, and now you have brought demons into our lives. We need all the help we can muster."

"I'm sorry," said Timoken. "I'll do what you want." He went back to the shelter and found Sila's little pile of flints. Taking the sharpest, he made his way to the stream.

"Now what?" the camel called after him.

"Rest, Gabar," Timoken grunted. "Tonight we work."

With his gift for multiplying, Timoken soon had enough willow stems to make two baskets.

The wizard was pleased with Timoken. Altogether, it had been a good day. A tangle of leaves, autumn flowers, and potent spells snaked through the trees. The wall was almost finished. When a misty dusk seeped into the forest, they stopped work and cooked the hare Eri had snared.

They were so hungry they hardly spoke as they ate. The fire crackled, bringing a warm blush to Sila's pale face. Lost in thought, she stared into the flames until Karli nudged her, asking, "What are you thinking about, Sila?"

She turned to him and said absently, "I was remembering our tree houses, and Tumi."

"D'you think . . ." Karli sucked on a thin bone as though it were packed with nectar. "D'you think the conquerors killed him?"

"No," Sila said sharply. "I told you, they'll make him their slave."

"Better to die," Karli muttered.

"Who is Tumi?" asked Timoken.

"A boy who was our friend," Sila said gravely. "He could swim, and he could catch fish like no one else." She glanced at Enid, dozing beside the camel. "Well, no one except her," she said, nodding at the dragon.

"What became of this boy?" Eri poked the fire and a shower of sparks lit the dark sky.

"When we left the tree-hides, he followed us," said Sila. "But the conquerors came with dogs, and we heard a scream. It must have been Tumi. There was nothing we could do."

Eri looked at Timoken. "They were looking for us. Those two brutes will be in trouble with Osbern if they don't catch us. The boy, Tumi, would have told them the direction these two took, and that they were following us."

"No!" said Sila vehemently. "Tumi was loyal. He was one of the bravest. If he told the conquerors anything, it would have been lies."

"But you think they caught him," Timoken said.

"Yes." Sila stared solemnly into the dark between the trees. "Can you rescue him, Timoken?"

"Perhaps." Timoken thought of his castle, of the task he had set himself. "But not tonight."

"Soon?" Sila begged.

"It won't be easy," Timoken warned her. "But if your friend is somewhere in Castle Melyntha, then I'll try. There are others in the castle who need rescuing."

Eri gave him a look that said *An almost impossible task, even with your skills.*

The wizard stood up and shook the hem of his long robe. "Must get a new one," he muttered. He unfastened the patterned gold brooch where it pinned his cloak at the shoulder, then he kicked off his worn leather boots. "We must all have a wash tomorrow," he said. "We smell worse than camels."

Sila and Karli grinned, while giving Timoken anxious, side-ways looks. He could have taken offense on Gabar's behalf, but instead he laughed, and they were free to giggle.

Eri banked down the fire, and one by one they went thank-fully to bed.

Timoken lay awake long after the others had fallen asleep. The wizard's snoring didn't seem to disturb Sila and Karli. They were tired, and slept deeply and peacefully.

A wolf howled somewhere in the distance — a real wolf this time, not a demon. An owl hooted, and wood mice scrabbled in the thickets. No sound came from the leopards, but Timoken knew they were close.

He waited until the tiny scrap of moonlight slipping past the door was at its brightest. Very slowly he sat up, then stood, tak-ing great care not to rustle his leafy bedding. Although Eri was snoring, Timoken couldn't be sure that an accidental snap or crackle wouldn't wake him.

But the wizard slept on. Timoken eased the door open, just wide enough to allow him through, then he hooked it shut again.

Creeping over to the camel, he stroked his nose. Gabar snorted and lifted his head. "What?" he said.

"Shh!" hushed Timoken.

It was too late. Enid, snuggling beside the camel, opened one eye. "What is it?" she asked.

"Go back to sleep," said Timoken.

Enid closed her eye.

"Gabar, get up. We're going to work," Timoken bleated softly in the camel's ear.

Gabar sighed, lifted his rump, and then stood.

Enid opened both eyes. "What are you doing?" she grunted.

Bending close to the dragon, Timoken murmured, "We're going to work, Gabar and I. But you mustn't move or make a sound. And don't tell the wizard."

"I can't. He doesn't understand me like you do." Enid spoke in a whispery kind of croak.

Timoken patted her head. "Go to sleep, Enid. We'll be back before morning."

The dragon obediently closed her eyes.

Timoken fetched the two willow baskets. Joining them together with long creepers, he hung them, one on each side of Gabar's hump. With a small leap, he flew up and landed between them. Regretting that he'd left the fur-lined saddle in Eri's possession (the wizard was using it as a pillow), Timoken made himself as comfortable as he could on the bony hump.

He had purposefully left the reins still attached to Gabar's head-harness, and, wrapping them around his wrist, he tugged at the hair on the camel's back. "Shall we fly?" he whispered.

Gabar turned his head to look at Enid.

"What's it to her?" said Timoken. "Anyway, she won't see."

"She might," said Gabar.

"So camels can fly as well as dragons. She'd be proud of you, Gabar. Come on, let's go."

He gave another tug on Gabar's rough hair and, slowly, the camel rose into the sky.

CHAPTER 12
Spirit Ancestors

The night was crisp and cold. A pale blanket of frost covered the trees and fields. Rivers and streams sparkled like melting silver. Timoken breathed deeply, inhaling the pure air of freedom. Sometimes, when he and Gabar were alone in the sky, he longed to stay in the air forever.

At last, they came within sight of the town. Timoken told his camel to land on the battlements of the nearest of the castle's eight towers.

"I'd prefer grass," said the camel. "Why the roof?"

"Because it's where we need to be," Timoken told him.

They flew on until they were above the castle. To Timoken's dismay there was a guard on the battlement of every tower.

"Now what?" snorted Gabar, rather too loudly.

The guard on the nearest tower looked up, lifting his spear.

There was nothing else he could do. Timoken instructed Gabar to fly above the tower and drop onto the roof.

"Not wise," grunted the camel. "Soldier."

"We'll have to make the best of it. Hurry up. We want to surprise him."

Obediently, the camel plummeted, like a stone, or perhaps a very large rock, down onto the tower.

The soldier gasped. He dropped his spear and his lantern. "Monster!" he murmured, and fainted clean away, which was exactly what Timoken had hoped for. Quickly, he bound the man's arms and legs with a few thin cords from his baskets. He hesitated before making his next move and then, having made up his mind, he tore a strip from the hem of the soldier's tunic and, removing the man's helmet, tied the cloth tightly around his head and over his mouth.

This gave Timoken an idea. He pulled off the soldier's chain-mail overshirt and placed it in a corner with the helmet and the spear.

"Is this what we came for?" asked Gabar.

"No," said Timoken. "It's extra."

The camel yawned. "I hope the rest won't take too long."

"So do I." Timoken looked around him at the high walls

of the battlements. There were deep openings at intervals all along the wall. Embrasures, as they were called.

Archers would loose their arrows from the embrasures, then dart behind a section of the wall before the enemy could hit them.

Timoken climbed into an opening and reached up. He could just touch the top of the wall. Running his fingers along the base of the highest block of stone, he felt the line of mortar that bonded it to the block below. Closing his eyes, he dug gently into the mortar. It moved beneath his fingers and he began to chant in the language of his homeland. The mortar turned to dust and trickled onto the roof. Timoken was so pleased, his chanting became a song.

The block wobbled. Timoken pushed it, and the great stone crashed onto the paved roof. Congratulating himself, Timoken set to work again. He paid no attention to the drumbeats filling the air. He thought the sounds were in his head. Behind him, Gabar made an odd, strangled sound, but Timoken took no notice. He carried on, pushing and singing, until at least a dozen red sandstone blocks lay scattered over the battlement. A whole section of the wall had now disappeared. With a whoop of joy, Timoken turned from his task—and almost fell back into the air.

He was surrounded by tall white-robed figures. They stood shoulder to shoulder against the wall; each one carried a spear, and their long brown arms shone with golden bracelets.

"My people," Timoken breathed.

They gazed at him, their wide, dark eyes glistening with life. And yet they showed no emotion. They stood silent and still, as if they were waiting.

"Spirits," groaned the camel. "Family, what have you done?"

"My voice must have called them," Timoken said in a hushed voice. "Perhaps it was the song, but I never asked. . . . My father sometimes spoke of our spirit ancestors, but I never saw them."

"You have now," the camel grunted.

They stood looking at one another, the twelve spirit ancestors, and Timoken and his camel. After several minutes had passed, Timoken ventured, "Why are you here?" Husky with reverence, his voice could hardly be heard.

In answer to his almost inaudible question, the twelve ancestors laid their spears against the wall and approached the blocks of sandstone. Timoken watched, his mouth agape, as each lifted a block and placed it on his head. Balancing the stones with one hand, they took up their spears with the other, and stood as before, waiting.

"Now what?" muttered Gabar.

Now what indeed. Timoken had no idea what he was supposed to do next. Slowly, it dawned on him that the ancestors intended to carry the blocks of stone wherever he wanted. If that was the case, then he and Gabar could carry more. Timoken set to work again, feeling and pushing, easing and pulling, until another six blocks lay at his feet. Putting three stones in each of the baskets hanging on either side of Gabar, he jumped on his back, saying, "Down to earth this time, Gabar!"

"If you're sure!" Gabar sailed over the wall and dropped to the ground. Fortunately, they landed outside the castle. A few lengths farther on, lantern light could be seen beside the great entrance, but the guards on watch neither saw nor heard the camel's swift descent.

"And now?" asked Gabar.

"Hush!" warned Timoken. He didn't know what to expect. He could only guess, and hope.

As he stared up at the battlements, he saw a movement on the wall, and then they came. One by one, the spirit ancestors fell through the air like a column of white birds, their bracelets and spears picking up the light from the stars like tiny fireflies.

"West," Timoken whispered in the camel's ear. "Where the thin moon sits on the forest."

Gabar began to walk down the hill. "Houses, Family?" he grunted.

"The town's asleep," whispered Timoken.

"If you say so."

Timoken looked behind him. The spirit ancestors were following. They walked in a line, their heads held high beneath the blocks of sandstone. When the camel reached the base of the hill, he walked on toward the town. The houses were dark and silent, and the cobbled road already dusted with frost.

The camel's feet padded on the cobblestones, but the spirit ancestors made no sound. In single file, they walked through the town and out into the forest, following the camel and the boy from the secret kingdom. The ancestors left no footprints, no trace of a scent, but now and then a thin sprinkling of red dust could be seen on the leaves and branches that they passed. . . .

The forest was a tangle of roots and thorns, and Timoken imagined that a long, long journey lay ahead; and then Gabar asked, "Why don't we fly? The stones are not too heavy for me."

Timoken smiled to himself. He waited for a break in the trees and then tugged the hair on the camel's back. Up they went, past the trees and out into the starry sky. One by one, the spirits followed, their white robes forming a long floating veil.

Gabar sailed over the forest, and when Timoken looked back,

he could see the spirit ancestors running through the sky, their feet treading air as though it were as smooth as desert sand.

They reached the cliff top that Timoken had chosen for his castle. Down went the camel and his rider, and down came the spirit ancestors. They landed in a row — and waited.

Gabar knelt on the hard rock. Wearily, he grunted, "Sleep, I beg. Do what you want, but leave me out of it."

Timoken lifted a block of stone out of the willow basket; measuring seven paces from the edge of the cliff, he laid the stone on the ground. One by one, he put the blocks in a straight line, then stood back and regarded his small wall with a frown of concentration. What next? Where to begin building a castle?

The ancestors had been standing as motionless as statues. Now they came alive and placed their blocks side by side, continuing Timoken's line. When they stood back, their wide mouths were closed, their lips didn't move, but a sound came from them: a deep humming, and from somewhere beyond the hum — drumbeats.

Timoken had always multiplied with his hands. "Why not my feet?" he asked himself. Leaping on the first stone, he began to sing. He ran along the line and back again, still singing. Eighteen blocks became thirty-six; thirty-six became seventy-two.

The line grew longer, the song became louder, and the drumbeats crescendoed.

"One hundred and forty-four," Timoken sang. "Two hundred and eighty-eight; five hundred and seventy-six; one thousand, one hundred, and fifty-two."

The thousand blocks multiplied. Their line snaked along the cliff top, edged through the sparse trees, and disappeared into the shadows. The line became a wall, two blocks, three blocks, four blocks tall. Higher and higher. The thin moon descended, and Timoken rested beside his camel. He laid his head against Gabar's warm flank and fell asleep.

When he opened his eyes again, the sun was up, but Timoken sat in shadow. He was staring at a red wall. His gaze traveled up the wall, high and higher. His eyes widened, he thought they might pop out of his head. For, standing before him was a great red castle.

Timoken stepped back, back, and back, until he nearly fell off the edge of the cliff. The castle loomed above him. It didn't resemble any that he'd seen on his travels through Europe, and it was not at all like Castle Melyntha.

Dizzy with astonishment, Timoken followed the great red wall as it stretched toward the sun. Facing south, he found two broad pillars, one on each side of a massive wooden door. Hardly believing what he saw, Timoken walked out into the trees. When he had gone some distance, he looked back, half expecting the castle to have vanished. It hadn't. What he saw kicked at his heart like a giant's foot. He was looking at a building with a domed roof and four steeply pointed towers. Apart from its color, the building was an exact replica of the palace where he'd been born.

He ran back to Gabar, his heart pounding. When he saw the camel, idly munching dry grass, Timoken cried, "Look! Look! Can you see?"

"I'm not blind," said Gabar.

"Did I build this in my sleep?" Timoken pointed at the great red wall.

"Hardly," said the camel. "The spirits made it."

"My ancestors"—Timoken sank to his knees—"from the secret kingdom."

The spirit ancestors had gone, leaving him with a home fit for a king. But who would live in it?

Timoken rocked back and forth. His dream had come true. The dream he had held for more than two hundred years, and now he knelt before his dream, too amazed and too fearful to enter it. "I must," he told himself.

He got to his feet and walked to the massive doors. He pushed and they opened. Inside was a courtyard paved with colored stones. Timoken crept across the glassy floor. Ahead lay five arches. He took the center arch and walked down a long passage. At the end was a room bright with painted walls and patterned carpets. A gold couch stood on a raised platform, and, in his mind's eye, Timoken saw his parents, sitting on their own golden couch, just as they had before their kingdom was invaded.

Timoken brushed away angry tears and ran out of the palace. He wanted to tell someone, he wanted to share his wonderful new home.

Leaping on Gabar's back, he urged the camel into the air. "We must find Eri!" he cried. "And Sila and Karli."

"Your family," snorted Gabar.

"Yes," said Timoken, happily realizing the truth. "But they could never replace you, Gabar."

"No," said the camel.

They flew above the forest and Timoken peered down through the trees. He saw the clearing, or thought he saw it, but the shelter had gone. "Down," he told the camel.

Gabar landed in an empty clearing. There was no sign that anyone had ever been there. No charred remains, no cut wood, no chewed bones.

Timoken slipped off the camel's back. A twig snapped, a bush rustled. Timoken swung around as a boy emerged from the trees. He was tall, with matted blond hair and a broad forehead lined with scratches.

"Shrivel my soul," said the boy. "It's the one with the fire in his fingers!"

CHAPTER 13
A Ruin

Y ou!" said Timoken.

"Thorkil," snapped the boy. "Rightful Earl of Holfingel."

They stared at each other, both frowning, and Thorkil's sister, Elfrieda, emerged from the trees behind her brother. She was
followed by several of the children Timoken had seen before.

"Why are you here?" asked Timoken.

"Why shouldn't we be?" Thorkil retorted. "This isn't your
forest."

"But your homes are in the trees," said Timoken. "Have you
left them for good? They were so well hidden."

"The leaves will fall soon," said Elfrieda in her hard, disdain-
ful voice. "We always abandon the tree houses in autumn."

"We can be seen in naked trees," added Thorkil. "You hadn't thought of that, I suppose."

Timoken noticed the dagger in the boy's belt. Thorkil's hand rested on the hilt.

The sight of it made Timoken's fingers itch. "There were many more of you," he said. "Are you all here, somewhere in this forest?"

"The others were caught," Thorkil said bitterly. "Edwin's brother was taken."

"My twin," said a boy with a long, narrow face. He had small, dark eyes and his thin hair was cut in a crooked line just below his ears. "Conquerors!" He spat the word.

"They were looking for you." Elfrieda stared accusingly at Timoken. "They saw us in the trees."

"When they began to throw their spears, we had to come down. Some of us didn't stand a chance." This was said by a boy with long, dun-colored hair. He wore a cap made of straw and feathers that looked very like a bird's nest.

"But you stood a chance, for you are here," Timoken said bluntly.

"Wyngate is speaking of the younger ones," said Elfrieda. "We have longer legs and we can run. The soldiers didn't bother to follow us."

"They caught enough children to work for them," Thorkil added bitterly. "My friends were too badly wounded to move. I had to leave them." It was clear that this distressed Thorkil, although he tried hard not to show it.

Timoken didn't know what to say. He wondered what had made Thorkil come to this particular forest when there were so many other directions he could have taken.

"We followed the coast," Thorkil said, almost as if he'd read Timoken's thoughts. "Now and again we saw the camel's foot-prints. Wyngate is an excellent tracker." He nodded at the boy with the bird's nest cap. "I had heard about the Deadly Sands and we avoided them. At the edge of this forest we heard laughter —"

"And singing," said Elfrieda. "I thought I recognized the tune. We followed the sound. It came from this very spot."

"But there was no one here." This was said in a quiet voice by a girl who peeped over Elfrieda's shoulder.

"Except you," said the boy beside her, grinning at Timoken.

They looked very alike, with their thick, dark hair and wide-set, hazelnut eyes.

Timoken judged them to be about twelve and thirteen.

"I'm Esga," said the girl with a smile. "He's Ilgar." She gave the boy a friendly poke.

"I'm called Timoken." He was about to introduce his camel when someone laughed, very close to his ear. He stared at the others. They had heard the laughter and looked equally baffled.

"What's going on?" Thorkil demanded.

"I'm not sure." Timoken looked up at Gabar.

The camel blinked. "Small family-boy," he grunted.

Timoken thought he recognized the laughter. Now he knew it was Karli. But Karli was nowhere to be seen. The others were peering into the trees. Thorkil strode about, kicking the under-growth. "It's that laugh again. We hear it, but we can't see it. Why?"

Eri's wall, thought Timoken. It had to be. He hadn't expected it to be so powerful. He was impressed, and then uncertain. What was he supposed to do? Somehow the spell-wall of leaves and flowers had made Eri, Karli, Sila, and the shelter invisible.

Thorkil gave up. He shrugged and sat on the ground. "Is this where you live?" he asked. It was clear that he expected Timoken to advise him about where to sleep and what to eat.

The others joined Thorkil on the grass and looked at Timoken hopefully.

"I sort of live here," Timoken admitted. "More or—" He was interrupted by a loud squawk and, looking up, saw Enid hovering above him. She was carrying a large fish in her jaws and appeared to be in some confusion about where to deliver it.

Thorkil and the others leaped up, some of them screaming.

"What *is* that thing?" cried Elfrieda, pointing at Enid.

"A dragon," said Timoken. There seemed to be no point in keeping the truth from them.

"Dragons don't exist." Thorkil sounded uncertain.

Let him think what he wants, Timoken decided. In a series of hoots and grunts he called to Enid, "I can't find the wizard."

"Don't tell us that you can talk to dragons," Elfrieda muttered.

Timoken saw no reason to argue. He was about to go in search of a gap in the spell-wall when Enid suddenly plummeted onto Gabar's hump. The camel gave an indignant yell. "Talons!" he bellowed, looking beseechingly at Timoken.

"Your claws are hurting my camel," Timoken told Enid.

The dragon curled her talons under her feet, folded her wings, and stared at the tree children with puzzled golden eyes.

The children were equally puzzled, and a little afraid. But they had seen so much that was horrifying and unbelievable, they were not easily daunted. In fact, hungry as they were, most of them showed as much interest in the fish as they did in the dragon.

"That's a mighty fine fish," Thorkil remarked.

"Enough for us all," said Esga.

"And some for tomorrow," added her brother.

"Make the dragon give it up!" Thorkil demanded, looking at Timoken.

"I won't make her do anything," said Timoken.

"Then we will." Thorkil strode up to the camel. "Come on, Edwin, Wyngate. Help me to get that fish."

"DON'T YOU DARE!" boomed a voice.

Thorkil stopped in his tracks. "Who said that?" he asked in a slightly shaky voice.

"I did." A floating mob of frosty hair materialized just below the camel's nose. A long, weathered face, with storm-cloud eyes and a silver-streaked beard, appeared beneath the hair and, suddenly, there was Eri. He looked younger, fiercer, and more impressive than he had before. It was as if, within his own spellbound wall, he had become a more definite wizard, not an aging, tattered man. His staff had acquired a pale and mysterious sheen that was reflected in the wizard's dark eyes.

Eri's sudden appearance caused a shocked silence. Even Thorkil's mouth fell open.

"So, you would steal my fish, would you?" Eri stepped close to Thorkil and scowled in the boy's face.

"I—I didn't know it was yours, sir," Thorkil stammered.

"But you knew it wasn't yours." Eri banged his staff on the ground and, immediately, Enid flew down and dropped the fish at his feet. Thorkil had already leaped back, and there was a gasp of wonder as the dragon spread her wings and soared up into the sky.

The group of children watched the dragon disappear above the trees and Wyngate murmured, "Where's it going now?"

"Not IT," said Eri sternly. "SHE. And she's going to get another fish, seeing as there's more of us for breakfast than she'd bargained for." He covered the fish with leaves and then counted the children's heads. "Eight. Hmm. So how many of you were captured?"

"Some died, sir," Edwin said. "Near twelve."

"Eleven," said Thorkil in a superior voice. "I taught them how to count, but they don't always get it right."

Edwin scowled, and Wyngate said, "I could count before I came to the forest."

"I asked how many were captured," Eri said impatiently. "I shouldn't have thought it a difficult question for one who teaches others to count." He stared at Thorkil.

The earl's son cleared his throat, thought a moment, and then said, "There were thirty-three of us, once."

"So twelve were taken," Eri said thoughtfully. He pinched his forehead.

Timoken was wondering why the wizard was so interested in numbers when a high, clear voice said, "But not us, sir."

Thorkil gave a start. "Sila?" he said, frowning into the trees.

"Step out, Sila," said Eri. "You, too, Karli."

As the two children materialized before them, Timoken observed how much brighter they appeared. Behind the spell-wall they had become what they might once have been, before the conquerors came. Sila had lost the dark circles beneath her eyes, and acquired a strong, confident look.

The other children seemed to notice the difference. Astonished by Sila and Karli's sudden arrival, even Thorkil couldn't find a word to say.

"Hullo, Thorkil," Karli said boldly.

Thorkil could only stare.

"So you couldn't save our friends," Sila said accusingly.

Thorkil shook his head.

Elfrieda was the first to find words. "I see that the wizard has worked his spells on you." She spoke with a familiar sneer in her voice.

"There's nothing a good dose of herbs can't cure," Eri told

her. "Now, we won't turn you all away, but you'll have to build your own shelters, and fast. I can feel rain coming on."

The tree children stared uncertainly at the wizard.

"Come on!" He thumped the ground with his staff. "Don't know how? Then look at this!" He took a few paces back, waved his shiny staff in the air, and murmured something incomprehensible.

Timoken watched as the shelter slowly took shape in the center of the glade. He noticed that a low wall of leaves and flowers had been laid all around the base. *A double wall of spells*, he thought. Eri wasn't taking any chances.

The children stared at the shelter, mouths agape.

"You'll need two of these." The wizard tapped the shelter's wall of wood and creepers. "Find one strong branch, straw, moss, ivy. You can see what's needed. Bring it all to us and my friend here will help you to do the rest." He turned to Timoken. "Agreed?"

Timoken gave the wizard a cool stare. He didn't want to reveal his skills to so many. He thought of the grand building on the cliff, ready to live in. There was no need to build more shelters, but he hadn't expected to share the castle with someone like Thorkil.

The wizard frowned at Timoken. "Well, are you going to help?"

Timoken said, "Yes," in a quiet voice.

"Off you go, then!" Eri waved his staff at the children.

Chattering excitedly, they plunged into the forest thicket. Thorkil was the last to leave. He looked over his shoulder and gave Timoken a puzzled look.

When they had all gone, Eri turned to Timoken and asked, "So, where were you, then, all night?"

"We were worried," said Sila. "Eri told us we must make a second wall, so that we would be invisible, but I said, 'Timoken won't be able to find us.'"

"And Eri said it was too bad," added Karli. "And that you should have come back before dark."

"True," Eri said gruffly. "I'm aware that you can look after yourself, Timoken. But I'd like to know where you were all night."

Timoken smiled at them and spread his arms. "I've built a castle," he said happily.

The response was not what he had hoped for. The wizard scowled at him, while Sila and Karli looked baffled and disbelieving.

"How could you?" said Sila. "In just one night?"

Eri slowly shook his head. "Did you have both feet in the realm of enchantments, Timoken, when you built such a wonder overnight? It sounds like a feat that will draw those other beings like bees to a honeypot."

"Can we sleep there tonight?" begged Karli.

"Are there feather beds and soft covers?" asked Sila.

"No!" exclaimed the wizard. "You shall not sleep in this — enchanted castle — until I have seen it for myself."

"You shall see it, Eri!" Timoken declared. "I'll show you tonight, and you'll be amazed."

"Hmm, we'll see. . . ." The wizard gave an unintelligible mutter and looked into the sky.

The next moment, Enid dropped into the clearing with an even larger fish than the first.

"Those children will be hungry when they get back," said Eri. "Build a fire, Karli, and we'll get cooking."

The tree children returned in twos and threes; they had gathered everything the wizard asked for. After laying their bundles in the clearing, they sat beside the fire and ate the fish that had been slowly roasting. They stuffed the flesh into their mouths as though the meal might be their last. Their eyes shone and their chins glistened with fish oil. They licked their fingers over and over, and some of them looked at the dragon, dozing in the shadows, and mouthed the words, "Thank you! Thank you, dragon!"

When they had eaten, Timoken took the branch they had provided and prepared it. The branch was gnarled and green with lichen, and it took him some time to smooth and shape it. He didn't want to work while they watched but he knew their curiosity was too great to avoid. And so he sat quietly and multiplied.

They watched in astonishment as the smooth posts rolled from under Timoken's hands. Gasps of wonder rippled around the group and, now and again, Timoken looked up and smiled at their compliments. He noticed that Thorkil looked puzzled and, somehow, defeated.

When the posts were ready, everyone helped to build the shelters. They finished just before nightfall. Hungry again, the children sat around the dying fire and Ilgar pulled a cooking pot out of the bag he had brought with him.

"That's a fine pot," Eri remarked.

Esga explained that they had kept the pot with them ever since they ran from the burning town. "It was our mother's most treasured possession," she said, "and we would rather have lost our lives than let the conquerors have it."

Eri looked at the pot with admiration. "Fine as it is, an empty pot's no use," he muttered, stroking his beard. "I want two strong boys to fill that pot with water from the stream. The rest of you find roots. Surely you know what's edible by now."

Ilgar and Edwin set off for the stream. Timoken followed Wyngate into the trees.

The boy with the bird's nest cap had a trustworthy look. Timoken liked him. When he found Wyngate alone, he asked him to come to the stream with him.

Wyngate grinned. "What d'you want of me, magic boy?"

"Come and see," said Timoken.

They ran together through the trees until they came upon Ilgar and Edwin.

"One pot is not big enough for all, don't you agree?" Timoken asked the boys.

"Not nearly," Ilgar said, putting it on the ground.

Timoken knelt beside the pot. They gathered around him expectantly as he ran his fingers along the lip of the pot, once, twice, three times. He put his arms about the pot, closed his eyes, and chanted in the language of the secret kingdom. Then, opening his eyes, he spread his arms wide and a cooking pot rolled away from him, and then another. The first still remained before him.

"Three!" Ilgar exclaimed.

Wyngate patted Timoken's shoulder, and Edwin said, "I wish we had met with you before, Timoken."

Timoken smiled, knowing he had made new friends.

They filled the three pots from the stream and carried them back to the clearing.

Eri chuckled when he saw them. He divided the skin and bones from the fish and put them in the three pots. Soon the other children began to arrive, carrying edible roots and berries already washed in the stream.

"Three!" cried Esga when she saw the pots. "Our mother would have been so proud."

They put their gatherings in the three pots while Eri stoked the fire. Timoken sighed. He knew there was something he must do. He leaned close to Sila and whispered, "I need to borrow your cup."

"I know why." She looked at the steam rising from the cooking pots and went to fetch her clay cup from the shelter.

"Eleven," she whispered, handing the cup to Timoken.

"I know." Still a little self-conscious about his multiplying, he stepped into the trees.

He remembered noticing a smooth-topped rock some way into the forest and made his way through the undergrowth. When he found the rock, he set the cup on it, gathered his thoughts — and hesitated. Something cold had touched his back.

Timoken pulled his cloak tighter and stared into the shadows. Nothing moved. "Sun Cat, Flame Chin, Star!" he said quietly.

The undergrowth rustled and three leopards' heads appeared above the tangle of thorn and scrub.

"We are here," said Sun Cat.

Timoken smiled with relief. "But something else is here, too."

"Yes," Flame Chin agreed.

"What is it?" asked Timoken.

"Other," said all three.

"Continue," said Star. "You are safe."

They stayed close while Timoken multiplied the cup. Taking off his cloak, he wrapped it around the cups and carried them back to the clearing. The leopards followed closely. He could hear the soft *swish* of grasses as they passed.

Emerging into the clearing, Timoken placed the twelve cups beside the fire. Some of the children clapped, and most cried, "Hooray for Timoken!" Thorkil gave him a grudging smile.

"Let it cool!" commanded the wizard, as the children grabbed their cups and leaned toward the cooking pots.

Eri wrapped leaves around the hot iron handles and removed the pots from the fire. "Count to twenty, slowly," he said, "then dip in your cups. The bones will sink to the bottom, but watch out." He glanced at Timoken. "We could do with a ladle. Any ideas?"

"Tomorrow." Timoken yawned. He felt almost too tired to drink the soup, but he forced himself, knowing he would be traveling that night.

When the pots were empty, the children stumbled wearily into their shelters. Four girls in one, four boys in the other. They each clutched a precious cup. Karli and Sila kept to their own beds.

Timoken and the wizard sat beside the glowing embers long after the others had fallen asleep. A cold mist had begun to seep through the trees. The fire died suddenly, and gray ash lifted from the blackened twigs.

"Time to go," said Eri.

"We'll get there faster on Gabar," said Timoken.

The sky was thick with clouds so Eri lit a rush that he'd dipped in fish oil. "I don't like starless nights," he said, "and we haven't had time to make leaf walls for the new shelters."

"Sun Cat!" Timoken called softly. "Flame Chin, Star!"

He was answered by three deep, rumbling purrs.

"All is well, then," said Eri.

The camel had fallen asleep and grunted irritably when Timoken woke him.

"Sorry, Gabar. We have to make another journey," he said quietly. To the dragon, dozing close, he whispered, "You're in charge, Enid."

"And what of those big cats?" asked Enid, her golden eyes flicking toward the trees.

"They are guardians, too," Timoken admitted. "But I need all of you to keep my friends safe."

"Agreed," she snuffled.

The wizard handed Timoken the flaming rush before they mounted. "I need to carry my staff," he explained.

With a resigned yawn, the camel stood up. "Flying?" he asked.

"Flying," said Timoken. "Back to my castle."

"Of course." Gabar sighed. "Where else?" and he rose into the air, gracefully avoiding the topmost branches, until he was safely above the forest.

They sailed through the clouds, the wizard relighting the rush every time the damp air killed the flame.

It was difficult to see through the mist but, at last, Timoken made out the sharp lines of the cliff. "Down, Gabar," he said.

The camel dropped onto the plateau and Timoken stared into the gloom. "It's too dark," he said, handing the rush-light to Eri. "You're taller than me. Can you raise the light higher?"

Eri stretched up his arm. "I'm holding it as high as I can, but I can see nothing," he said.

"The light's too bad," cried Timoken. "The castle is here, right here, I know it is."

As if to contradict him, the clouds suddenly parted and a thin moon shone down on the land directly before them.

Timoken passed a hand across his eyes. He couldn't believe what he saw.

All that remained of his beautiful palace was a tumble of red stones. A ruin.

CHAPTER 14
The Damzel of Decay

Is this your castle, Timoken? I fear you have deceived yourself."
The wizard approached the tumbled ruin and poked it with
his staff.

"My ancestors built it," Timoken admitted. "But it *was* a
castle."

"Ah, ancestors," said Eri. "They can be unpredictable."

"They built a castle," Timoken insisted. "They helped me
to carry the stones and I multiplied them in hundreds and
thousands, and then I fell asleep. When I woke up, there was
a castle here."

"A dream, Timoken."

"NO!" he cried. "It was real. I walked through it. I found a
room like the place where my parents used to sit."

"Ah. Even more I see it was a dream, Timoken. While you slept, you dreamed of your old home in the secret kingdom." The wizard turned his back and walked around the pile of stones. "Where did they come from, boy, these fine red stones?"

"Another castle," Timoken confessed.

"You stole them?"

"From a conqueror's castle," Timoken said defiantly. "When I saw the people's houses, so small and dark in the castle's shadow, I thought of the cruelty they had to endure, and I wished I could have destroyed every bit of that castle."

Eri chuckled. "No doubt. But let us hope the conquerors don't come looking for their stones." He put his hand on a section of the wall and immediately stepped away. "What's that?" He looked at his hand. "There's fungus here; the stones are disintegrating."

Timoken touched a stone. It felt icy cold and crumbled under his fingers. "Ugh! What is it, Eri?"

"Get away from it!" the wizard cried. "Those forest fiends have worked their sorcery here."

Timoken leaped back.

"I've come across their evil mold before." The wizard raised his staff and roared at the stones. He used ancient words that

Timoken had never heard and couldn't understand. But there was no mistaking the wizard's next command.

"GO! GO!" Eri's ringing tones carried over the ruin and deep into the forest. He brought his staff cracking down on the pile and Timoken's spirits rose. Surely the wizard's deep, fierce voice would banish any sorcery.

They waited while silence fell. Behind them, the camel shifted uneasily. A breeze drifted around them, smelling of decay. The clouds obscured the stars again and Timoken lifted the rush-light, just to make sure the castle hadn't reappeared. But it was still a pile of decaying stones and he felt an urgent need to leave the place.

Suddenly, Gabar gave a deep, rumbling bellow. "Leave, Family! Leave here!" the camel implored.

Timoken couldn't move. He stood frozen to the spot while, beside him, Eri murmured, "Too late. It's here!"

A pale cloud lifted from the ruin. It hovered above the stones, gradually assuming the faint outline of a woman. Eri drew in his breath as the figure became clearer. A moment later, a woman stood before them, on the highest stone. She had a young, moon-like face; her hair was white and fell in long strands to her waist. Her eyes were colorless, and her loose robe the greenish-gray of a stagnant pool.

Frightened as he was, Timoken found a voice. "Did you destroy my castle?"

"Destroy?" Her voice had a rough, sticky croak.

"There was a castle here," Timoken said boldly. "But the walls have crumbled, just in a day. Did you do it?"

The woman gave a heartless smile; her eyes remained cold and empty. She stretched out a hand, saying, "Give me your lovely cloak, and you'll have your castle back."

"Never!" cried Timoken. "I'll keep my cloak and get my castle back, in spite of all your sorcery."

The woman's eyes turned black. She opened her bloodless lips and a dreadful shriek came out of her. All at once, she was in the air and flying at Timoken, her arms stretched before her, her black-tipped nails pointing at his throat. She was almost on him when Eri struck her with his staff, and down she came with a dreadful, gurgling screech.

She wasn't long on the ground. As she flew up she gave three blood-chilling shrieks and the ruin trembled, sending stones in all directions. Pale forms rose out of the ruin: They were smaller than the woman and less defined, their features barely visible in their white moonfaces. They came at Timoken and the wizard with a deafening high-pitched wailing, their green-gray arms twisting and waving.

The wizard lashed out with his staff, Timoken with his flaming rush. He felt their fingers in his hair, tearing at his neck, tugging the cloak. With one hand, he pulled his cloak tighter. "Stay with me," he told the cloak. "Defend yourself."

There was a hiss of pain as the fiends began to feel the sting of the cloak. Six of them flew up, nursing their injured hands. They twisted about and made for the camel, who had no way of defending himself. They pulled his ears, sank their claws into his back, bit his neck, and covered his eyes with sticky veils of green-gray fungus.

Gabar's bellow of fear and pain filled the night air and traveled far over the forest.

Timoken ran to defend his camel but the fiends clutched Timoken's hair and tugged him back. "Eri!" called Timoken. "Help Gabar, I beg you."

The wizard was in no position to help. It was all he could do to keep the fiends from scratching out his eyes. As soon as he had dashed one of the creatures to the ground, another landed on his shoulders. "I can't, Timoken," he gasped. "He'll have to save himself."

Timoken watched, helplessly, as Gabar dropped to his knees. "Family, it is the end," he groaned.

Standing high on the ruin, the woman's gray lips were drawn

into a hideous grin. Her pale eyes observed the battle before her with satisfaction.

A vicious bite on the leg sent Timoken tumbling to the ground. The fiends hovered above him, their dreadful voices momentarily quiet. In the brief interval between their screechings another sound could be heard. A distant squawk that came closer and closer.

All at once, a great winged form plummeted out of the air. Long tongues of flame shot from the beast's nostrils and her steely talons hit the ground with a loud, metallic ring.

"Enid!" breathed Timoken.

The dragon made straight for the creatures that were attacking Gabar. With one puff of her fiery breath they fled, shrieking with pain, their longs fingers smoldering. Gabar bellowed his joy and stood up, shaking the nets of mold off his eyelids.

Enid's bursts of flame reached far into the shadows. She swung her head about and the fire caught at every fiend. Their toes, their ashen hair, their long fingers, and their white floating robes; all were singed and burning in a moment. Screaming with agony, the vicious creatures rose into the air and vanished. Only one remained, the moonfaced woman. Her mouth twisting with fury, she faced the dragon and shrieked, "Reek and Mildew, Mold and Stinkweed eat you away; I am the Damzel of Decay!"

Timoken and the wizard watched Enid nervously, wondering if she could withstand the woman's curse. The dragon looked puzzled. She lifted one clawed foot uncertainly; her flames died and a single puff of smoke issued from her nostrils.

"She wanted the camel killed," Timoken shouted to Enid. He was about to add, "Us, too!" But with a roar of fury and a huge burst of flame, Enid rushed at the moonfaced woman.

In a second, the Damzel had gone. Where? They couldn't tell. The dragon stood on the ruin, her tail lashing the air, her hot breath sweeping the fungus that covered the stones, and they began to steam.

"Thank you, Enid." Eri approached the dragon and she jumped down and wrapped her scaly wings about him. But even while she hugged the wizard, Timoken could see that she had eyes for no one but the camel.

Gabar gazed back at her. "Tell the dragon," he grunted. "Tell her, thank you."

"Gabar the camel is grateful for your help," Timoken told Enid. "You saved his life."

"It was nothing," said the dragon. "A great pleasure to protect such a noble friend."

"She said it was a pleasure," Timoken told Gabar. He didn't think it necessary to relay the whole message.

Before they left the cliff top Timoken went to examine the stones. The pile where Enid had been standing was still warm. The stones didn't crumble when he touched them. He ran his hand across more and more of the stones. They were firm and solid. It was as if Enid's breath had hardened them, like clay in a hot kiln.

Timoken called the wizard over and asked him to touch the stones. When Eri had felt their warm solidity he scratched his forehead for a moment and then said, "The Damzel of Decay. Hmm. It's my belief that the Damzel and her minions grow the rot and damp and feed off it, just as a farmer grows his corn to feed his family."

"What a disgusting idea," said Timoken.

"But think what it means, boy. If we can keep this place dry and warm, if we keep fires burning and Enid plays her part, the Damzel won't come back."

"And we can build the castle again," Timoken said hopefully. "Because there *was* a castle here. Do you believe me now, Eri? Do you?"

"I'm beginning to," said the wizard. "Now, let's get some sleep."

They climbed on Gabar's back and, with Enid flying beside them, traveled through the sky and down into the forest clearing.

Only two shelters could be seen, the third was shrouded in invisibility. At a touch of Eri's staff, however, the vanished shelter appeared, with the two children inside it still sleeping peacefully.

The following morning, Timoken woke up to find that Thorkil had already built a fire and Elfrieda had gone with the others to look for breakfast.

Timoken sat beside the fire and held his hands out to the flames. The sun had barely risen and the air was cold. The ground felt damp and an icy dew dripped from the trees. Timoken hunched his shoulders and looked into the forest, almost expecting to see the Damzel.

Thorkil came and sat beside him. "I saw you return," he said, glancing at Timoken. "I couldn't sleep, and when I looked out of the shelter I saw your camel dropping from the sky." He frowned. "But he has no wings."

"No," Timoken agreed. "I can make him fly."

"I see." Thorkil stared into the fire. "And you can fly, too, and speak the camel's language, and the dragon's. You can multiply and . . . and what else can you do?"

"I can bring storms and make them go."

Thorkil grimaced. "So what are you, Timoken?"

"I'm an African with one foot in the realm of enchantments.

If you stay with me, you'll always be at risk, because the attention I get is often dangerous." Timoken hadn't meant to say so
much and he added, "You can believe me or not."

Thorkil hunched closer to the fire. "My mother would have
believed you. She was very superstitious. But my father would
have needed proof. He told us there was nothing to fear from the
carved demons on the church wall or the paintings of the end of
the world. He was a very practical man."

"How did he die?" asked Timoken.

"He lost his head."

"Mine, too."

They had something in common, and that caused them to
smile wistfully at each other. Timoken hoped it wasn't just a
temporary truce.

Soon after the other children arrived with their cups of
nuts and berries, Eri appeared carrying a dead hare. Thorkil
wanted to know how had he managed to catch it. Eri told him
politely, "Like anyone else. Not by magic if that's what you
think."

After breakfast Eri stood up, brushed the remaining crumbs
from his robe, and said, "I have something to tell you all."

They fell very quiet. Fingers were licked silently, cups placed
carefully on the ground.

"Timoken and I are leaving this place," Eri told them. "We are going some distance away, where a castle will be built. Don't frown, my friends. You already know that Timoken is a magician, and I have some skill, too."

There was a murmur of agreement.

"There are dangers attached to this boy." He pointed at Timoken with his staff. "Demons follow him: witches, fiends, monsters; he draws them all, but he has plenty of strengths to fight them off." He paused and looked around the group. "So if you come with us, you know what to expect."

"Where else can we go?" asked Elfrieda.

"Stay here," said Eri. "You can obviously look after yourselves." He turned abruptly and went into the shelter.

Karli and Sila were already packing up their few possessions. Sila took one of the kettles and pushed it into her bag. Timoken put the stolen armor in one of Gabar's panniers and saddled him up with the hareskin cushion.

The tree children were in a huddle, talking softly among one another. Wyngate looked over his shoulder and grinned at Timoken. Elfrieda's voice rose above the others. "We should stay here, where we're safe. Who knows what trouble the African will lead us into?"

There were some anxious mutters, but Timoken sensed they

were waiting for Thorkil's decision. At last he said, "I'm going with Timoken and the wizard."

Elfrieda scowled at her brother, but Wyngate said, "Me, too." Edwin said, "And me," and Ilgar and Esga cried, "Yes!" The other children quickly agreed.

Timoken realized he would have to lead them and so, with Gabar grumbling along beside him, he set off through the thick undergrowth of the forest. Eri walked behind him, with Enid sometimes taking off into the trees and sometimes stumbling over rocks and thorn bushes, but all the time sending little puffs of smoke into the air, to keep the damp at bay.

Sila ran to catch up with Timoken. "Will the castle keep us safe?" she asked him.

"I believe so," he said.

"And when it's built, will you rescue Tumi and the other children, so that we'll all be together again?"

"I'll try."

She seemed satisfied with this.

It took them all day to walk through the forest. By the time they reached the river and the great cliff beyond it, they were aching with hunger and exhaustion.

"Where next?" called Elfrieda from the back of the procession.

"Over the river," said Timoken, "and up to the top of the cliff."

The children crowded together on the riverbank. They stared at the wide expanse of rushing water, and Thorkil said, "And how do we do that?"

"I'll have to carry you, one by one," said Timoken. "Maybe the dragon can help."

"If you want to sit on spikes," grumbled Elfrieda.

The others looked at Timoken. They had never seen him fly.

"So, who's first?" Timoken looked along the line.

Just as Wyngate stepped forward, there was a sound from the cliff above: a whining howl, and then a bark.

"Back!" hissed the wizard, raising his staff. "Into the trees, quickly."

They ran into the trees, Timoken tugging Gabar's reins, Eri waving Enid away from the river.

"Don't make a sound," Timoken warned the camel in a hushed grunt.

"Look!" whispered Eri.

At the edge of the cliff stood three soldiers, their helmets glinting in the last rays of the sun. Behind them, braying and barking, was a pack of great black hounds.

CHAPTER 15
In Castle Melyntha

The bakehouse was the warmest place in Castle Melyntha. On cold mornings, the stableboys would sneak into the steamy room and hunt for crumbs of bread. The baker would shoo them away if he saw them, but if they got a chance they'd be back, crawling behind the long table as a tray of loaves was pulled from the oven, and snatching at loose scraps from the hot bread waiting on the table.

"You're like a plague of ants," the baker would shout good-naturedly as he hauled the boys out and shoved them into the courtyard.

One morning, Tumi managed to avoid the baker's eagle eye. He was crouching under the table, right at the far end where the shadows were deepest, when two soldiers came in. Tumi could see their boots and the tips of their scabbards as they moved around the table.

"We need more loaves today, Edgar," said one of the soldiers.

Tumi recognized the voice. It was Aelfric, the man who had caught him in the forest.

"How many more?" asked Edgar.

"Ten, at least. A troop has just arrived from Ravenglass."

"Ravenglass Castle?" said Edgar. "That's some distance away."

"Stones have been taken from their battlements," said Aelfric. "The watchman said it was a spirit riding a monstrous beast."

"They came to warn us. We'll have to keep an eye on our own battlements."

That surely had to be Aelfric's friend, thought Tumi. *Yes, it was definitely Stenulf Pocknose.*

"Stones?" Edgar pulled another tray from the oven. "Why would a spirit steal stones?"

"Ah!" Aelfric gave an unpleasant chuckle. "We don't think it was a spirit, do we, Stenulf?"

"We do not." Stenulf's voice rasped in his thick throat. "We think we know who's stealing stones. Now, who rides a monstrous beast? Remember Timoken?"

"Timoken? 'Course I do. He escaped, didn't he, after allegedly killing one of his own friends?" Edgar moved up and down the table, putting out the hot loaves. One of his feet came danger-ously close to Tumi. The boy pulled in his knees and held his breath. "Don't believe the story myself," Edgar went on. "He was a nice lad, Timoken."

"You'd better believe it." Aelfric began to pile the hot loaves into a crate. "Who else could get a monstrous beast to fly? Remember what our guards saw? A flying camel."

"They found a track of red dust leading into the forest," said Stenulf. "They're putting the hounds onto it. Ravenglass hounds are famous for their tracking."

"But if the camel flies . . . ?" said Edgar.

"Those dogs can find a scent even in the air," Aelfric retorted.

"Famous for it," Stenulf repeated. "And you know how camels stink."

The two soldiers marched out of the bakehouse carrying their crate of loaves.

Edgar's feet were still for a moment, and Tumi heard the baker mutter, "Stones? What would he want them for?"

Tumi thought of Sila. She had followed the boy and his camel. Knowing Sila, she would have found him. Sila was an extraordi-nary girl. She never gave up. Tumi missed her company almost as much as he missed his fisherman father and his patient, hard-working mother. Before he could stop himself, he let out a sigh.

Edgar peered under the table. "Ant!" he growled. "You'd better get back to the stables before those soldiers see you."

Tumi scrambled out and scampered for the door, but just before he left, Edgar, feeling a twinge of pity for the half-starved boy, called, "Here!" and threw him a hunk of bread.

"Thank you!" Tumi mumbled gratefully as he took a bite. He hid the rest of the bread up his sleeve.

Where to eat without being seen? There were guards everywhere. They'd send Tumi to the stables and he'd have to share with all the other boys. He crept along the side of the wall, past the well, and on to the stock house, where all the food was stored. The door was open. Tumi couldn't believe his luck. The guard's back was turned, he was bending over and adjusting the cord on his boot. Tumi slipped behind the guard and into the dark storeroom.

Immediately inside, he began to stuff the bread into his mouth. He was so hungry he hardly bothered to chew, and almost choked on the last piece. His stomach rumbled loudly and he was sure the guard would hear, but the man was now talking to someone.

Tumi leaped behind a large barrel just as the cook and his assistant came in. They began to move sacks of grain about. As they got closer to Tumi, he crept around the barrel and behind another, standing beside it. All at once, his heel came into contact with a hard object. A foot? Tumi lost his balance and fell back onto something soft. Maybe a body? There was a slight grunt from the person underneath him.

"What was that?" said the cook.

"You moved too many sacks," said his assistant. "Look out, that crate's going to fall."

His warning came too late. A crate toppled from the top of a pile, sending apples rolling over the floor. One came so close to Tumi's hand, he could have touched it.

The cook swore softly. "Pick them up, Rolf, quick as you can," he told his assistant. "I want to get this flour to the kitchen as soon as possible. A hundred pies they want tonight."

Throwing apples into the crate, Rolf asked, "Why so many?"

"We've got company," said the cook. "Ravenglass men."

The crated apples were left on the ground, and Rolf heaved the sack of flour onto his back. Still grumbling, he followed the cook out.

Very slowly, Tumi rolled sideways. He and the body were wedged tight between the barrels and the wall. In the dim light of the storeroom he could just make out the features of a youth with a wispy mustache. He had very pale blue eyes.

"Who are you?" whispered the young man.

"Tumi!"

"Never seen you before."

"Nor me you," whispered Tumi. "They caught me in the forest."

"A rebel?"

"I suppose. Why are you hiding here?" asked Tumi.

"My friends brought me here. Safest place they could find. It's a long story. Get off me, will you. I've got a hole in my chest."

Tumi crawled backward and stood up behind the first barrel. The boy got to his feet and rested his elbows on the other barrel. He was very tall and his arms were thick and muscular.

With his eye on the open door, the youth whispered, "I'm Mabon. I'm supposed to be dead. My family gave me a funeral, but I wasn't there. They buried a bundle of rags."

Tumi didn't understand. "Why?" he asked softly.

"Can't explain. It's too complicated. Can you help me get out of here?"

Tumi looked at the shadowy outlines of the sacks, the barrels, and the crates. He stared at the narrow window high above them, and last of all at the broad back of the guard who stood before the open door. "How?" he whispered.

"Throw an apple," Mabon suggested. "The guard will be

distracted. While he goes after it, you run out in the opposite direction. He'll see you and give chase, but you'll have the advantage. I'll slip out while he's running after you."

"He'll catch me," said Tumi.

"Maybe not."

"I'll do it if you take me with you when you escape from the castle, because that's what you're going to do, isn't it?"

Mabon's pale eyes held Tumi's gaze for a moment. "What's your name again, little rebel?" he asked.

"Tumi. Swear you'll take me with you."

"Hush." Mabon looked at the door again. "We'll take you, but I don't know how we'll do it."

"Swear you'll try."

Mabon took a breath. "I swear. Go on, now. Throw that apple. Soon as the guard moves, run out."

Tumi stole across to the crate. He took two apples. Keeping one firmly clutched in his left hand, with his right, he threw the other apple past the guard.

"Hey!" To Tumi's horror, instead of following the apple, the guard strode into the storeroom. Tumi leaped out of the way just as the man thrust out his spear. As he bounded for the door, Tumi saw Mabon duck behind a barrel, and then Tumi was in daylight and running for his life. He could hear the man's heavy feet thudding behind him, and then someone flew past him, racing toward the guard.

There was a sudden yell of anger and a thump. The running footsteps ceased.

Looking back, Tumi saw the guard getting to his feet. Beside him stood a boy with bright copper-colored hair. He waved Tumi on.

"Forgive me," Tumi heard the boy say. "I thought I saw a rat." He rubbed his foot. "No harm done."

"You ran into me on purpose!"

Tumi ran on while the guard continued to roar at the boy. "You'll be sorry for this, you poet's son. Times are changing."

When Tumi rushed into the stables, Siward, the head stableboy, shouted, "Where've you been, you shirker? We've ten more horses to deal with."

"W-why?" Tumi slumped into the straw, trying to get his breath back.

"Ravenglass horses," said one of the other boys. "There's a troop of soldiers come to pay a visit."

Tumi dragged himself to the far end of the stable. He was glad that he was dressed like the others, in a coarse tunic and scratchy hose. Hopefully, the guard wouldn't spot him. The other boys still called him "seal-breeches," even though his sealskin breeches were now his pillow.

A black stallion gave Tumi a defiant look as he approached him to remove the harness. "It's all right, I'll give you a good rub-down." Tumi stroked the glossy black nose.

The stables rang with the sounds of whinnying horses, shout-ing boys, clanking pails, and jingling harnesses. But the guard's loud voice carried above it all: "Which of you boys has been stealing apples?"

"None of us has had time to steal apples," Siward replied indignantly. "We've been run off our feet all morning, grooming the Ravenglass horses."

The guard swore and turned on his heel.

The stableboys were always loyal to one another. Trust counted for more than getting into the guards' good graces. Tumi hid his apple under the straw in the corner of the stall. He would give it to Siward later—after he'd taken a bite himself.

It was a long morning. At midday, the stableboys gathered in the courtyard for bowls of thin soup and a meager scrap of bread. They had the same meal in the evening. Siward was pleased with his apple. "Well done, seal-breeches," he said. "Pity you couldn't have got more."

When they'd fed and watered the horses, the boys curled up

in their familiar places in the straw. One lantern was left burning, and a guard paced the cobblestones outside the stable door.

Across the courtyard, a feast was taking place in the great hall. Music and singing could be heard, and then voices were raised as the drinking got under way. Louder and louder came the drunken shouts — benches crashed back, tankards rolled onto the flagstones, arguments turned ugly, and now and again there was a clash of steel.

Tumi slept at last. He dreamed that he was back in the tree-hide, sharing an apple with Sila.

"Rebel, wake up!"

Tumi opened his eyes. Still half-asleep, he could just make out the face peering down at him. It was the youth from the storeroom.

"See, I've kept my promise," whispered Mabon. "But come now, quickly."

Tumi was suddenly wide awake. He scrambled to his feet, curling the sealskin breeches around his neck. He crept after Mabon, past the sleeping stableboys and the horses snoring in their stalls. The boy with copper-colored hair stood just inside the door. "Hurry!" he whispered.

Outside, a guard sat on the ground with his back against the wall. His head drooped onto his chest and his tankard lay on its side, a pool of beer beside it.

The copper-haired boy put a finger to his lips and then turned and began to run.

Mabon and Tumi followed him around the wall, past the well, and across to a narrow door set in one of the towers. Beside the door, another guard lay sprawled on the cobblestones, an empty tankard still in his hand. He was snoring like thunder.

The copper-haired boy knocked on the door very softly, three times. At the third knock, the door was opened and they stepped into the tower.

A woman stood before them, holding a lantern. She had dark skin and was not young, but Tumi thought her very beautiful. Her smile, when she saw him, was warm and welcoming.

"And who is this?" Her voice was deep and tuneful.

"Someone who helped me," said Mabon. "A rebel's son."

"Tumi," said Tumi.

The woman repeated his name thoughtfully. "An interesting name. And I am Zobayda."

"Princess Zobayda," said the copper-haired boy, causing Zobayda to laugh softly. "Let's get going," he continued, leaping up the narrow steps.

"Edern is always in a hurry," said Mabon.

Zobayda lifted the lantern and began to climb, beckoning Tumi to follow her. Mabon came last. His breathing sounded harsh and labored as they climbed higher, and Tumi heard him stop several times. What was it he'd said about a hole in his chest?

Zobayda covered the lantern as they passed through a room where several people lay sleeping. Tumi could only see vague outlines beneath the bedcovers, and then he was climbing another set of steps. When he reached the top, he found himself in a room where three elderly women sat beside a fire. It seemed as if they had been waiting for something, and their smiles were wide and excited.

"All is ready," said the oldest, who was, indeed, so old that her eyes and lips could hardly be seen among all the deep wrinkles of her face. She was surprisingly agile, however, and moved swiftly to the wooden shutter at the window. Opening the shutter, she revealed a knot of linen tied to an iron hook below the sill.

"The wolf has gone," said the old woman, patting the knot. "Who's next?"

"Us," said a voice.

Tumi looked toward a third set of steps as a boy stepped down into the room. He was carrying a baby in his arms. A hareskin cap covered the top half of the boy's face, but his mouth and chin could be seen. His lips looked very dainty for a boy.

The baby had mysterious eyes; they were a dark, stormy, gray and looked too knowing for a child.

"Come on then, Beri," said the old woman.

Beri handed the baby to her and leaped onto the sill. Grabbing the knot of linen, he said, "Put the baby on my back. He'll be quite safe. We've been practicing."

The baby was gently secured onto Beri's back. He put his little arms around the boy's neck and they disappeared from view.

"You!" The old woman nodded at Tumi.

When he went to the window, she said, "Wait till she's down."

"She?" said Tumi.

The other two women giggled, and Edern said, "Beri likes to dress as a boy; she finds it easier to ride in breeches."

The old woman peered over the sill. "She's down now. Come on, you."

Tumi obediently swung himself over the sill, grabbed the knot, and, with his feet, found another knot in the long rope of cloth. As he climbed down, he could feel lengths of velvet and silk beneath his fingers. It seemed that the women had made a rope of their best clothes.

At last he was down. The girl, Beri, stepped to his side and whispered, "Whoever you are, you'd better come with me. The others will follow."

"Tumi," he said.

"Tumi, then. Come on." She slipped into the darkness, saying, "It's steep here. Watch out."

Her warning came almost too late. The castle was built on a hill and the north wall of the Widows' Tower stood almost directly on the edge of the steepest part of the hill. Before Tumi knew it, he was sliding, stumbling, and rolling over grass, rocks, and thorns. He could hear Beri above him, moving more carefully. The baby didn't make a sound.

Tumi rolled the last few paces. He landed in a heap before a startled horse. A lantern was swung in his face and a wolf looked down at him. No, not a wolf, a boy with teeth like a wolf, and a surprised grin.

"Who are you?"

"Tumi." He got to his feet. "Mabon brought me."

"Oh, well. You'll have to ride with him, then," said the boy. "I've only got four horses."

Edern stumbled into the lamplight. Grabbing the harness of one of the horses, he said, "Well done, Peredur," and mounted quickly.

Zobayda arrived, still calm and elegant after her uncomfortable descent. Edern held out his hand and Peredur helped her up onto the saddle in front of Edern.

Mabon arrived at last, breathing heavily and clutching his chest. He coughed several times and laid his head against his horse's neck before climbing into the saddle. "Come on, Tumi, you're with me," he said, extending a hand.

Tumi felt himself being shoved upward from behind. He swung himself onto the saddle before Mabon, and looked down into Peredur's wolfish grin.

"All ready, then?" said Peredur, mounting his horse.

"Where's Beri?" asked Zobayda.

"She's off," said Peredur. "Always liked to be first, didn't she?"

"The fish, the wolf, the eagle, the bear . . ." Mabon began.

"The burning sun, and the running hare," said Edern.

Tumi was puzzled. "What does all that mean? Is it a secret code?"

"They're our emblems. We'll tell you about them later." Mabon chuckled. "Let's go."

They set off behind Edern and Zobayda. Ahead of them, Peredur followed Beri.

"How did you get the horses?" asked Tumi, still utterly confused by all that was happening.

"We have friends. Britons who can hide where the conquerors can't find them. When our prince was killed over the sea, my father died with him, and so did Peredur's. Our families have left the castle now; my friends stayed until I had recovered from my wound. But now we're all free. Hoorah!" Mabon patted the horse's rump and they began to gallop.

They were soon in the forest, and that was where everything began to go wrong.

There was a sudden shout, and then a scream. Edern's horse bolted and Tumi saw two mounted soldiers, their spears pointed at him and Mabon. Beneath one of the soldier's helmets, a broad pocked nose could be seen. Stenulf.

Mabon's horse reared up and Tumi felt a sharp blow on the side of his head. He slipped out of Mabon's grasp and slumped forward. Before he lost consciousness, he thought, *If I'm not dead yet, I soon will be.*

Minutes later, Tumi opened his eyes to find he was still astride the horse. Mabon was breathing heavily in his right ear.

"What happened?" mumbled Tumi, rubbing his head.

"Branch hit you," said Mabon. "We scattered when the soldiers appeared. I thought those two brutes were sleepy with drink."

"Aelfric and Stenulf?"

"Yes. Them. They're the worse of the lot."

An eerie cry echoed through the trees. It sounded like an eagle's call.

"Edern," said Mabon. "It's his special call. It's the nearest he can get to flying." He gave the horse a light kick and they cantered toward the sound.

They could scarcely see where they were going. The moon was thin and the stars obscured by clouds. They were almost upon Edern and Zobayda before they realized it. Edern had stopped calling, and Zobayda had extinguished the candle in her lamp.

"Is that Beri?" Zobayda whispered.

"No, it's us," said Mabon.

"Where is she?" Zobayda said anxiously.

"I'm sorry, Zobayda," said Peredur. "I think they caught her."

"What?" she cried. "We must go back and rescue her."

"It's too late, Princess," said Peredur. "We'd never get close. But she won't be harmed."

"She will! She will!" moaned Zobayda.

"No, Peredur's right," Edern said gently. "Beri will be safe. They won't dare to hurt her. There's a rumor that Osbern D'Ark wants her to be his wife."

"You stupid boys. D'you call that safe!" Before they could stop her, Zobayda had slipped down from the horse and run into the trees.

CHAPTER 16
Black Hounds

Timoken heard a shout. It wasn't carried on the air, but came from somewhere deep inside his ear. He drew his cloak tighter and, bending his head, he murmured into its crimson folds, "What am I hearing?"

The jinni's spirit seemed to stir. No sound came from the cloak but an image appeared before Timoken. He saw the jinni's face on the ring his sister had worn. He saw Zobayda running through the trees and calling: The name she called was Beri.

Timoken felt his shoulder being violently shaken.

"What's the matter with you, boy?" came the wizard's harsh whisper. "We must go back."

Timoken blinked. For a moment he had almost forgotten the soldiers and their dogs. From the safety of the trees he looked up at the cliff top. The soldiers were still there, staring down into the forest. Could they see him?

"Come back, Timoken!" Eri tugged his arm. "Do you want a spear through your heart?"

"The cloak protects me," muttered Timoken.

"What's happened to you?" The wizard tugged again.

"I saw my sister," whispered Timoken.

"You saw her in your mind. Let's leave this place."

"No." Timoken stared at the pack of black hounds pacing and growling behind the soldiers.

A low howl came from Timoken. The wizard let him go and stepped away.

Timoken's howl carried up the steep cliff: "Go home," he told the dogs. "Go back to your warm kennels, your dinner bones, your crying puppies. Go, before it is too late!"

The leading hound lifted his head and began to whine. It sounded almost like a human sobbing. The rest of the pack joined in and soon the air rang with the whining and whimpering and squealing of dogs. The soldiers shouted at the pack, ordering them to be silent, but the dogs weren't listening. They bounded away, back through the forest, following their leader home to Ravenglass.

Believing their hounds had caught another scent, the soldiers mounted their horses and rode after the dogs.

Timoken smiled with satisfaction. "They won't be back for a while," he said.

The wizard scowled. "And what then?" he grumbled. "We'll never be able to defend our pile of stones against an army."

Karli and Sila came creeping out of the trees. "But, sir," Karli said, "you can make another magic wall."

"Yes, Eri," said Sila. "You can make our castle vanish, can't you?"

"It isn't even a castle," muttered the wizard.

"It will be," Timoken told him.

The other children began to emerge from the trees. They gathered around Timoken and the wizard, questioning and chattering in low, urgent voices.

"What shall we do now?" "Will the soldiers come back?" "How can we build a castle?" "Where will we sleep tonight?"

Timoken put his hands over his ears. "Aaargh!" he growled. "Be quiet. I can't think."

"We are not as loud as you, Timoken," said Thorkil coolly.

"Quiet, everyone!" Eri lifted his staff and the voices dropped to an occasional mutter.

Timoken's hands fell to his sides. "We are not going to let the conquerors stop us from building our castle," he said.

There was an enthusiastic murmur of agreement. Elfrieda was the only one to raise a question. "As I said" — she glanced at Enid — "I refuse to go up there" — she pointed to the tumble of stones high above — "sitting on a row of spikes. So how are we going to get there?"

"Like this!" Timoken seized Elfrieda round the waist, lifted her off the ground, and carried her, screaming and kicking, over the river and up to the top of the cliff.

"You brute!" shrieked Elfrieda as Timoken dropped her gently on the ground.

Laughter from the children below made her angrier than ever. She raised her arm, ready to strike Timoken, but he bounded out of reach, climbing up the pile of stones with light, half-flying leaps. Elfrieda scrambled after him, yelling, "You won't get away with this, you rude, ignorant oaf!"

Timoken danced around the top of the pile while Elfrieda pulled herself up, falling back as the great stones shifted beneath her, now clawing herself closer to the top. And then, at last, she was there. She lunged at Timoken, he leaped back and, all at once, he was rolling down into darkness. With one long terrified wail, Elfrieda rolled beside him, until they reached the bottom of a stony slope.

Timoken rubbed his eyes. It wasn't so dark after all. The ground was soft, like a carpet. He got to his feet. A low lamp was burning on a distant table. Beside him, Elfrieda sat up with a groan.

"What happened?" she moaned.

"We fell through a hole."

"I gathered that, but how can there be a . . . a room under all those stones?"

Timoken shrugged. He looked about him. He saw carpets on a far wall, their colors muted in the dim light. He saw a couch covered in cloth of gold and silken cushions; he saw a marble floor veined in gold: his parents' golden room. "It's still here," he said.

"What's still here?" Elfrieda stood up, rubbing her bottom.

"The castle," said Timoken. He stared up at the circle of light at the top of the slope. "It was only the outer walls that crumbled, and the four towers. They were much higher than the roof. They just fell on top of it."

"And through it," Elfrieda pointed at the rubble lying on the rug where they stood.

"But it won't be so difficult to rebuild," said Timoken.

"Huh!" was Elfrieda's only reply.

They crawled carefully up the ramp of fallen stones and climbed out of the opening. As soon as they appeared, there was a cry of relief from the crowd far below.

"We thought you were gone!" shouted Eri.

"The castle's still here!" Timoken replied happily. "Underneath all this!" He kicked the stones beneath his feet. "But we can live here while we build."

Elfrieda gave a long sigh that the others never heard.

Leaving Elfrieda to grumble, Timoken flew down to pick up the others. First came Sila. When Timoken returned for the next, Eri said, "Enid's spikes are not so sharp on her neck. If you sit just behind her head—" He beckoned Enid and she ambled over to him. The wizard pulled himself up to sit on her neck. Adjusting his robes and wincing very slightly, he said, "Girls might have to sit sidesaddle, like me; boys on the other hand . . ."

"I'll try," said Karli eagerly.

"You next, then, Karli!" Eri clicked his tongue twice and, flapping her wings, Enid carried the wizard over the river and up to the top of the cliff.

Two of the new girls, Aldwith and Azura, looked uncertain. "That didn't look comfortable," said Aldwith. Azura agreed.

But when the dragon came back, Wyngate, Edwin, and Ilgar were all eager to take their first ride on a dragon, and so was Esga.

Karli climbed on. "It's good," he called as Enid carried him aloft. "Her spikes don't hurt, they're kind of springy."

Azura and Aldwith weren't convinced. They waited for Timoken.

Night was falling fast and starlight cast few shadows. When all the children had been carried to the cliff top, they stood looking down at the forest. The excited chatter that had followed their first experience of flying had been replaced by an awed silence. Below them, an immense sea of trees reached to the horizon, a dark world that merged with the infinity of a sky studded with distant mysterious stars. The children who had lost everything knew without even looking at one another that their lives had changed. They had taken an enormous leap into the unknown, into a life on the edge of enchantment.

"Let us go beneath," the wizard said quietly.

"This way." Timoken began to climb the pile of stones. "Be careful," he warned as he took light steps across the top of the ruin. "Ah, here it is!" he exclaimed as his foot found the edge of the opening.

"Don't go too fast," said Elfrieda, "or you'll be rolling over boulders all the way, like I did."

As each one approached, Timoken took their hands and let them slide gently into the hole, and then down the stony slope into the room below. When they were all inside, he bounded deftly over the ruin until he could see Gabar standing below.

"D'you want to come up?" Timoken called softly.

"Dragon and I are staying here," Gabar replied.

"Good night, then, Gabar." As Timoken turned away he suddenly remembered something. With one leap, he was in the air and flying down to the camel.

"I thought you had forgotten," said Gabar as Timoken removed his saddle and the baskets hanging on either side of him.

"I had," Timoken admitted. He slipped off the bridle of the camel's harness, saying, "There, you'll sleep better now."

"Mm." The camel trotted into the trees where the dim shape of a dragon could be seen, her head lowered in sleep.

Timoken took the baskets and the hareskin saddle back into the room below the rubble. They were all waiting for him. Most of them stood in a group, uncertain what to do next. Thorkil and Elfrieda had wandered to the far end of the room. Here, the soft light from the lamp played on the rich colors of the carpets hanging on the wall: Timoken remembered those carpets and he remembered the lamp, casting its glow on his parents' smiling faces. But who had kept the light burning? Were his spirit ancestors still close?

The wizard walked over to the couch. He sat down, placed the plump silk cushions at one end, and laid his head on them. Lifting his feet onto the couch, he bid them good-night and closed his eyes.

The children stared at the sleeping wizard.

Karli said, "I'm hungry."

Timoken took a handful of nuts from one of the baskets and began to multiply, too tired even to talk; the others sat in a circle and passed the nuts round. The sound of cracking shells echoed through the golden room. Timoken wondered what his mother and father would have made of it all. He could sense their presence, feel their gaze upon him. Before the tears came to his eyes, he found himself smiling.

One by one, the children left the circle and found a place in the room where they could sleep. Timoken was the only one left awake. He took out the helmet that had belonged to the Ravenglass soldier and began to multiply. He worked on until he had two hundred helmets, then he began to multiply the spears. When he had completed one hundred and fifty-nine, he fell asleep.

Three hours passed before dawn light spilled past broken beams and down the sloping shaft of stones.

Timoken woke up. He could hear movement in the room behind him. He rolled over and saw the wizard tapping the row of helmets with his staff.

"What's all this, boy?" Eri gave Timoken one of his disapproving stares. "Are you trying to make soldiers of these poor children?"

Timoken yawned and sat up. "No, Eri. But the Ravenglass soldiers might come back."

"Oh, they will. No doubt about that." Eri scowled. "They'll want to know what's going on here. If the king gets to know of a new castle in his realm, he'll send an army."

"So you'll make a spell-wall for us," Timoken said brightly. "And no one will be able to see our castle, ever, unless you want them to."

"What d'you think I am?" Eri said crossly. "It would take a week to make a place like this invisible." He waved his staff about and stamped his foot.

The children began to wake up. They gazed at their new surroundings, now becoming clearer in the morning light. Some had forgotten how they came to be there. When they saw the line of helmets and the pile of spears, they became even more confused. The wizard's angry voice unsettled them and they moved together for safety.

Thorkil woke later than the others. Immediately, he was on his feet and demanding to know how so many helmets had found their way into the castle. "Have you killed an army and hidden their bodies?" he asked Timoken.

Timoken grinned. "Nothing like that!" He told them where he had gotten the first helmet, and then explained why he had made so many.

Eri sat on the golden couch and listened with a disgruntled expression.

"We must move the stones on the roof, so that they form a sort of wall," said Timoken. "A wall with openings, like the battlements on the conquerors' castles. In every gap, we'll place a helmet with a spear beside it."

"Yes!" cried Wyngate. "And if the conquerors come, they'll think there's an army here."

"They'll send for reinforcements," Thorkil objected. "And then what hope would we have of keeping our new home?" He looked at the mound of rubble, and added, "Such as it is."

"Then I'll bring a storm," said Timoken.

They stared at him for a moment, disbelieving, and then Thorkil said, with a half smile, "I bet it will be a mighty storm at that."

Eri got up from the couch. "I need the girls," he said. "All of them, to find meadowsweet and gorse, rowanberries, willow herb, ground elder, flowering nettles, dame's violet . . . come on!" He began to climb the tumble of stones; Sila followed him, then Esga. The two other girls, Azura and Aldwith, looked at each other and then at Elfrieda.

"You heard the wizard," said Elfrieda. "Let's go. We can find breakfast on the way."

This seemed to cheer them up and they eagerly climbed after her.

When Eri and the girls had gone, Timoken led the boys onto the roof. It would be dangerous work, he realized, looking at the mounds of large red stones. At any moment a pile of them might drop through the roof, taking one of the boys with them. If only the spirit ancestors were here to help, but Timoken wasn't sure how to call them, or even if they would do what he asked.

"Watch your feet," he warned as he began to heave a stone off the top of a pile.

It was hard work. The Ravenglass stones were heavy and difficult to maneuver into place. But by midday they had built a wall of stones facing east, where the soldiers had come from. The wall ran the whole length of the castle that lay beneath. As they sat back, rubbing their aching hands, a delicious smell of cooking wafted up to them.

Eri emerged from the trees and looked up at the rough wall that rose out of the rubble. "Well done," he called. "Enid has brought you a meal."

They scrambled down and stuffed the cooked fish into their mouths, careless of the bones and almost choking on the skin. Enid had brought four fish today. Eri was proud of her. He kept his eye on everyone, just to make sure they all had their fair share.

After their meal, the boys had strength only to build another half of a wall. Timoken chose the south side, above the entrance with its great carved doors, now hidden in the rubble. Snatches of Eri's chanting carried up to them on a wind that was freshening every minute, as the sun began its slow descent.

The girls returned with fingers stained by leaves and flower stems. Elfrieda carried a large bundle of herbs bound together with ivy. After another meal of fish-bone soup, they clambered, shivering, into the golden room, and there Timoken sat and patiently multiplied Sila's hareskin blanket. By the time he had finished, some of the children were already asleep. The wizard helped

Timoken to cover them, and then climbed onto the couch and began to snore.

For a while, Timoken stared at the flickering oil lamp. Where had the oil come from? Who had lit it? There could only be one answer. The Damzel of Decay might have disturbed his ancestors but she hadn't entirely banished them. They were still here.

Life continued in the same way for three days. At the end of the third day, a rough wall had been erected all around the roof of the tumbledown building. Before they went to bed that night, Timoken and the boys placed the helmets in the gaps between the stones. Beside the helmets they laid the spears, their metal tips pointing outward.

When Timoken returned, he found the wizard lying on the couch. Eri seemed utterly exhausted. Timoken brought him a tankard of water and he drank it thirstily. "A pity this isn't the water of life, eh, boy?" Eri's storm-cloud eyes flashed briefly and then he gave a long sigh. "This task has all but stolen my life away," he said, "and the wall is not yet finished."

"Tomorrow, we'll all help," said Timoken.

"Tomorrow," sighed the wizard. "That's as may be," and he closed his eyes.

Timoken had one more task. He took the chain-mail tunic out of the basket and began to multiply. When he had ten tunics, he wrapped himself in his cloak and lay down. He pressed his cheek against the carpet that his bare feet had touched more than two hundred years before, and he fell asleep.

A little before dawn, the castle shuddered, and the wizard woke up. He could hear a thunder of hooves approaching from the east.

"Not ready! Not ready!" muttered the wizard. He dragged himself off the couch and went to wake Timoken.

CHAPTER 17
Ravenglass Soldiers

They're coming!" shouted Eri.

Timoken already ached from three days of lifting stones, and the wizard's violent shaking made him groan with pain. He rolled over, clutching his shoulder.

"They're coming," roared Eri. "Wake up. We must defend ourselves."

The other children were all awake now. They scrambled to their feet, rubbing their eyes, yawning and grumbling.

"Up! Up!" commanded the wizard. "Man the battlements. Take care not to be seen, but throw those spears as accurately as you can."

"First the chain mail." Timoken pointed to the pile of dimly gleaming tunics. With dazed expressions, the children pulled them over their heads, and Timoken led them up the ramp of stones and out onto the roof.

"Where's your armor, Timoken?" called Sila.

"I have my cloak," he said. "Keep your heads down. We don't want them to know we're children."

"Or get an arrow in our skulls," muttered Thorkil.

They could hear gruff voices, the jingle of harnesses, and the snorting and stamping of many horses. Timoken took a quick peek around one of the helmets, and his heart sank.

A long row of mounted soldiers was emerging from the trees on the eastern side of the ruined castle. They were well prepared for battle in chain mail, breastplates, and helmets. Swords hung from their belts, and those that did not carry shields or spears were armed with long bows and sacks of arrows.

"Are there many?" asked Eri, on his hands and knees behind Timoken.

"A great many. Perhaps two hundred."

The wizard closed his eyes and shook his head. "Too many," he muttered.

The wizard's choked voice made Timoken shudder. He hadn't known such a moment of doubt for a long time. In the heartless gray light, Eri looked old and utterly exhausted. He appeared to have lost all the youthful strength that he had gained behind the first wall of spells. And he was not wearing any armor.

Timoken watched the others crawl across the stones and crouch behind the empty helmets. He wondered why he had brought them all to this place. They could have lived safely in the forest for the rest of their lives. What had given him this restless yearning for a castle?

An arrow flew over Timoken's head and embedded itself between two stones. This was not a time for reflection. Bent double, he ran to the nearest spear and hurled it at the enemy below. There was a loud bellow, and a rain of arrows came out of the sky. The children hugged the walls. Not one of them screamed. They glanced at the fallen arrows, seized their spears, and flung them.

In answer, a cloud of arrows darkened the sky. The children flattened themselves against the stones and then each ran to seize another spear as the lethal arrowheads fell behind them.

Timoken raced from one helmet to another, hurling spears into the enemy below.

But he had a horrible suspicion that they were falling uselessly to the ground. He began to wonder if it was only the stationary helmets that were deterring the soldiers from climbing up the stones. Soon they would realize that the two hundred helmets were empty.

A few moments later, Timoken's fears were realized. Peering through one of the openings, he saw that some of the soldiers had dismounted; with drawn swords, they were now approaching the mountain of stones.

"We only have twelve spears left," Thorkil shouted. He too had seen the advancing soldiers.

"Keep throwing!" cried Timoken.

Thorkil seized a helmet and, pushing it on his head, stood up and aimed his spear at the leading soldier. There was a gurgle of pain and the man dropped to the ground, the spear embedded in his neck.

Encouraged by Thorkil's success, the other boys began grabbing helmets and dropping them over their heads. Barely able to see beneath the oversized headgear, they bravely stood and hurled their spears.

"We are about to lose our castle and our lives, Timoken." The wizard was sitting with his back to the wall, breathing heavily. "I hope you have a solution."

Timoken had already taken off his cloak. He climbed to the center of the ruin where the red stones were piled highest. Standing tall, he swept the cloak through the air above his head, and in the language of the secret kingdom, he called to the sky. He begged the clouds to batter his enemy with hailstones the size of pebbles, with bolts of lightning, with a wind strong enough to steal their helmets, and thunder that roared like a monster from the underworld.

"Go below!" he shouted to the others. "Now!"

They needed no second telling. The urgency in Timoken's voice sent everyone clambering down to the room below.

"The forest gods be with you, Timoken," said Eri as he followed the children.

The first soldier's head appeared above the wall just as the hailstones began to fall. Two pebble-sized blocks of ice landed on his helmet, and he disappeared without a sound. By the time the second soldier showed his face, the wind was so strong it tore him away and dropped him in the trees.

The storm raged above Timoken but never touched him. He flew over the pile of stones, chanting in his ancient language. And then his voice was drowned in thunder and the sky became darker than a night without moon or stars.

The soldiers were trying to remount when the lightning struck. Rods of blinding light crackled through the black clouds, striking helmets, spearheads, and breastplates, turning them into white-hot metal. The men were screaming now; they tore off their burning armor, and those that could still move lifted their wounded comrades onto the backs of their horses and galloped into the safety of the trees.

Timoken put his cloak around his shoulders and watched the last soldier disappear into the forest. He decided to let the storm rage for the rest of the morning, forcing the Ravenglass soldiers to retreat until they were too far away to change their minds and return to the attack. There was no doubt in Timoken's mind that they would return, for they had seen the great pile of Ravenglass stones, and their overlord would want to know how and why the stones had been taken to such a hidden and isolated place.

Leaving the stormy roof, Timoken went down to join his friends. He found a scene of great distress and confusion. Eri was burning herbs in one of the cooking pots, and a strange pungent smell filled the room. Beside the wizard lay a boy with a face of ivory; Elfrieda knelt over him, pressing a cloth against his shoulder. The cloth was slowly turning bloodred.

"What . . . ?" Timoken began.

"Thorkil has been wounded," Elfrieda said accusingly.

"How?" Timoken sank to his knees at Thorkil's feet.

"An arrow pierced his chain mail," said Eri. "No one noticed because he pulled it out, but now he is bleeding very heavily."

"He is dying," sobbed Elfrieda.

"Not if I can help it!" Eri put another bunch of herbs into the cooking pot and fanned the smoke over Thorkil's face. Timoken saw that the boy was breathing, but color was still draining from his face, and although his eyelids fluttered, he seemed incapable of opening them.

Swinging off his cape, Timoken threw it over Thorkil's motionless body, pulling it up to cover his face.

"What are you doing?" cried Elfrieda. "He can't breathe." She snatched a corner of the cloak, but Timoken put his hand firmly on her arm.

"Leave it!" Timoken commanded. "Your brother's life is ebbing fast; if you want it to return, you must allow the cloak to bring it back before it is too late."

Elfrieda frowned. She looked at Eri, who said, "Do as he says, Elfrieda. You can see that my remedy is of no use here." The wizard poked his charred herbs with a stick, his face weary and troubled.

Elfrieda sat back and allowed Timoken to adjust the cloak so that it covered every part of Thorkil, except his feet. The others crouched in corners, weak from the battle. Thunder rumbled overhead and the room was lit by constant flashes of lightning.

The gloomy atmosphere was relieved by Enid, who dropped

two fish into the opening. Karli scrambled up to fetch them. Eri cooked the fish over a low fire of straw and twigs. He glanced at Timoken as the flames began to scorch the ancient marble floor, but Timoken hardly noticed; he was too worried about Thorkil.

After their meal, everyone slept except for Elfrieda and Timoken.

"Will this storm never end?" Elfrieda moaned. "My head aches with the noise." She stared reproachfully at Timoken. "You brought the storm. Can't you stop it?"

Timoken's thoughts had been with Thorkil. He had become used to the thunder growling away above them. He looked at the cloak but dared not remove it. "I'll see what I can do," he said.

Climbing out into the storm, Timoken thought of the words he had so often used to bring thunder and lightning, rain and wind. He had always had the cloak with him when he called, and he had used it again to pacify a storm. Could he calm this turbulence without his cloak? He thought of arcs of color filling the sky. He thought of ancient words from his secret kingdom, words that were used to describe a rainbow. He shouted them at the black clouds and closed his eyes.

The hail that had been pounding the red stones turned to a gentle rain. The thunder faded and Timoken felt the sun on his face. When he opened his eyes, the black clouds had rolled away and a rainbow was growing through a vivid blue sky. When it had completed its arc, another appeared above it, and then another above that.

"Come and see the rainbows!" called Timoken. "Wake up, everyone. We have an omen to lift our spirits."

Sila was the first to appear. Still rubbing her eyes, she crawled onto the roof and looked into the sky. With wide, astonished eyes, she gazed at the three rainbows, crying, "Three! I've never seen three rainbows."

The others crowded onto the roof behind her. They pranced over the stones, happy to see the blue sky again, amazed to find three rainbows. Elfrieda and the wizard stayed below.

"It's a sign, isn't it?" said Karli. "It means we're going to be safe now, and perhaps Thorkil will get better."

Timoken wasn't sure, but he felt that a few moments of hope couldn't do any harm.

"They'll be back," muttered Eri when Timoken returned. "The soldiers. Curiosity is a powerful force. Their overlord will want to know all about this place. He'll send a message to the king, and there'll be an army out here . . ."

"But, Eri—" Timoken began.

"Hush!" the wizard said irritably. "They won't see anything, of course, because by then I will have finished the wall."

"We'll help," said Timoken, noticing the wizard's sagging shoulders.

"Naturally." Eri looked at the motionless form beneath the red cloak. "He's very still. I wish I could have done more."

"Your herbs stemmed the bleeding and kept him alive," said Timoken.

"For how long?" Eri poked the ashes in the cooking pot.

"We can't tell yet. But have hope, Eri. There are three rainbows outside."

"Hmm. You did that, Timoken. Don't tell me that you didn't."

Timoken couldn't deny it. He wished Elfrieda could have seen the rainbows, but she had fallen asleep beside her brother. "The forest is safe now," he said. "I'm going to gather food."

Eri nodded, but he didn't move. "I'll stay with these two," he said.

The others were eager to explore and followed Timoken down the stony mound and into the trees. They hadn't gone far when Enid came flying after them. Landing beside Timoken, she squawked, "Your camel is cross. He turned his back on me."

Timoken felt a rush of guilt. He had almost forgotten Gabar. Leaving the others, he flew down the cliff face and over the river. Gabar was sulking. He turned away from Timoken and refused to be lifted up the cliff.

"Please don't be difficult," said Timoken. "I've been very busy this morning."

"Difficult?" snorted the camel. "I have never been difficult. You have a large family now, and a camel counts for nothing."

"You and my sister have been my family for longer than any other beings on earth," Timoken said sternly. "Never forget it."

A low rumble came from the camel, and then he grunted, "I won't forget it, Family."

"Then, shall we go?"

"I hope you don't have to bring on storms like that too often," said Gabar, and he allowed himself to be lifted over the river, up the cliff face and into a sunlit glade in the trees. Enid came rushing to his side, and Timoken left them, smiling at each other.

The rainbows faded but the sun remained. While the others ate outside in the warm air, Timoken took some food to Eri. Karli followed with a pot of water. Elfrieda was awake but Thorkil hadn't stirred.

"He's breathing," said Eri, "but only just."

Elfrieda stared hard at Timoken. "We used to fight," she said. "But he's my brother, and I can't imagine life without him. Tell me he won't die."

Timoken took a chance. "Thorkil won't die," he said.

Elfrieda's smile told him that he'd better be right.

Before the sun went down, everyone was inside the ruin. They fell asleep while the sky was still light.

Timoken awoke to the sound of an owl. He remembered the night birds that used to sing in the secret kingdom. Before he knew it, he was chanting in his ancient language. The words and his gentle hum became a call to his ancestors. Beneath the sound of his voice, he heard a distant drumbeat. He stopped chanting and lay still. The sound of drumbeats intensified, but none of the others woke up.

A moonbeam lit the ramp of tumbled stones that led out into the night. As Timoken stared at the moonbeam, a group of white-robed figures suddenly appeared in the opening. When they stepped down into the room, their golden bracelets glinted in the moonlight, but their sandaled feet made no sound on the red stones.

Timoken held his breath as the spirit ancestors moved about the room. Silently, they whirled their spears above their heads, and the colored images that he remembered so well began to appear on the crumbling walls around him: birds and trees, pale flat-roofed houses, monkeys and flowers, lions and fish and proud golden camels.

The ancestors glided past Timoken, and out into the night. He couldn't stop his eyes from closing, but as he lay half-awake and half-dreaming, he felt the carpet and the marble floor move gently beneath him. He felt the room swaying, very slightly, and heard a muffled rumble just above him. The sound went on and on and on, a rumble that was almost musical, and he drifted into sleep.

"Wake up, Timoken! Wake up! Wake up!"

The voice was loud and insistent. Timoken didn't want to wake up. He wanted to stay with his dreams; his mother's face had been so clear, the palace in the secret kingdom so warm and splendid.

"Look! Look!" cried Sila.

Timoken rubbed his eyes. Sunlight was streaming into the room. Everything was bright. The walls shone with color. Was he still dreaming?

"You have your castle, Timoken." Eri stood looking down at him. "Or should I say, your palace?"

Timoken sat up. Thorkil was crouching beside him, drinking from a tankard. He grinned at Timoken and held out the red cloak. "This belongs to you," he said. He was still wearing his bloodstained tunic but he appeared to be completely recovered.

Timoken got to his feet. He gazed around the room. At the far end, a row of pillars led into a sunlit courtyard. Long windows were set into the colored walls on one side, and at the other

end, opposite to the pillars, five passages could be seen beyond
the five great archways. Each passage had a floor of bright
mosaics.

"Is it all . . . ?" Timoken whirled around and stared at the
ceiling.

"Complete?" said Eri. "Only you would know. This building
seems more African than British."

"But we've explored," said Karli, his face pink with excitement, "and there are many rooms smaller than this, but with
beds and tables and chairs and couches."

"And a grand entrance with doors as tall as five of us standing
on each others' heads," said Sila. "And the doors are all carved
out with pictures of birds and beasts and flowers and fish."

"And four towers," said Wyngate, "with pointed roofs."

"And no hole," added Esga, pointing to a corner where the
tumble of stones had been replaced by a smooth, gold-patterned
ceiling and, below it, another splendid couch, covered in cloth
of gold.

Timoken moved through the room in a daze. The palace was
a replica of his home in the secret kingdom. He went out into
the courtyard and climbed the steps to the roof. He stood on the
very spot where he had seen his father ride out to his death, and
where he had found that he could fly, on his last day in the secret

kingdom. He ran down the steps and through the courtyard. He wandered down every passage and into every room, and then he went out through the splendid doors of the entrance, while Eri and the others followed at a discreet distance.

"It is complete!" said Timoken, staring up at the massive doors. The carved creatures were just as he remembered them.

"Your palace, Timoken," said Sila.

"Our palace," Timoken corrected her. "Our home."

They grinned at him and some repeated, "Our home."

"And now we'd better hide it," said Eri.

CHAPTER 18
Vanishing

Everyone followed Eri out into the forest. It wasn't an easy task to find all of the flowers and herbs he wanted. The special plants were often hidden in brambles and thick undergrowth.

Sila led Timoken to the end of the line where he laid his stalks of willow herb. The wall was only ankle-deep, but he could already feel its potency: When he placed his feathery flowers on top of Sila's rowanberries, a soft warmth brushed his fingertips and, for a fraction of a second, his fingers felt weightless, as though they were not attached to his hand at all.

"You felt that, didn't you?" Sila beamed at him. "Imagine what it will be like when we're inside our castle!"

Timoken couldn't imagine. "What happened when you were in the vanished shelter?"

Sila wrinkled her brow. "It was like floating in a glass bubble."

Timoken looked back at the castle. How would it feel to stand in such a large vanished building? he wondered. He thought he could hear the distant crack of a falling tree, but dismissed it as one of the many sounds a forest makes.

Esga and Ilgar arrived with bundles of ivy and dried meadowsweet. The boundary of plants grew and grew. They had to go farther and farther into the forest to search for the plants that Eri demanded. Wyngate found another cliff face, where gorse clung to the rocks and flowering herbs grew in the fissures.

The wall was almost finished when Enid came flying out of nowhere. "Men!" she screeched. "Many. Horses. Many, many, many." Now the sound of falling trees made sense to Timoken. They were cutting a way through the forest big enough for an army.

He had just carried an armful of herbs around to the edge of the cliff behind the castle.

Even though a steep cliff and a river should have kept them safe, Eri wasn't taking any chances.

"Here! Drop it here, Timoken!" The wizard pointed with his staff. A gap of only one stride was left to fill. Sila and Karli ran up with bunches of herbs. Thorkil arrived with a branch of rowan-berries. The wall was complete.

"Into the castle!" barked Eri. "Now. At once. All of you."

They did as he asked. It was extraordinary to walk through the grand entrance of their new home, rather than scramble up into the trees, or climb a mound of rubble. Timoken went to fetch Gabar.

"I'm invited inside, am I?" said Gabar.

"Of course. It's your home," Timoken told him.

"Very nice," the camel remarked as he was led past the tall carved doors, and he kept repeating this as he walked through the room of colored walls, stopping briefly to give the golden camels a critical glance. "Very nice indeed," he said as he strode into the sunlit courtyard.

The wizard had not appeared, and Timoken ran to see what had become of him. The sound of a vast approaching army couldn't be ignored.

"Go back!" Eri told Timoken. "My task is not yet finished."

"But, Eri —"

"Go!"

The wizard's tone was so compelling, Timoken dared not

disobey him. He left Eri standing between the castle entrance and the wall of leaves and flowers.

Inside the castle, everyone gathered in the golden room and listened to Eri's chanting. His powerful voice carried through the thick walls and resounded around the castle. It took on the sounds of the forest: a song that might have been made by wind in the leaves, or a waterfall, the beat of wings, the humming of bees, or the stealthy footfalls of a deer.

And then came the other sounds, drowning the wizard's voice. The thrum of hooves and the shouting of men.

"What will they do to Eri?" cried Karli.

"They won't catch him," said Timoken.

"What if he doesn't finish the spell?" Elfrieda muttered.

"He will," said Timoken firmly, though he didn't feel as confident as he sounded.

There was a bang at the end of one of the passages, the sound of running feet, and then Eri bowled into the room, his silver-streaked hair standing on end as if stiffened by frost, his beard full of twigs, and his gray eyes flashing like a thundercloud. "Done!" he declared, and collapsed on the couch.

What followed was stranger than anything Timoken could

have imagined, and that included his first ride on a flying camel. As the roar of the army outside intensified, the walls of the castle began to thin. Horses and men could be seen through a veil of fine rain, a mist that glinted with droplets of silver. The mist dissolved until nothing remained between those inside the castle and the army outside — nothing but a sheet clearer than glass.

Timoken held his breath. How was it possible that the army couldn't see him or the castle? Their commander rode back and forth in front of his troops. He called out three names and three soldiers rode forward. The commander drew his sword from its scabbard and pointed it at the castle; the tip of his sword seemed to be aimed directly at Timoken. The soldiers frowned. They were the men who had first discovered the ruin. Others, behind them, had been caught in the storm. With eyes wide and incredulous, they stared at the empty space that had once been filled with a mountain of red stones.

"How can so many stones disappear?" shouted the commander.

"We don't know," came the mumbled answer.

"Are you sure this is the place?"

"Yes, my lord," answered one of the soldiers.

"Maybe not," said another.

"Perhaps it was somewhere else," said the third.

The first man shook his head. "It was here." He rode forward, blinking beneath his deep helmet. Others moved up behind him. They came closer; now they were in the courtyard. The camel grunted as horses walked past him, but his grumbling voice was lost in the clatter of hooves and the creak of armor.

The mounted soldiers moved through the castle toward the cliff edge and a wave of panic caused Timoken to sink to his knees. He put his head down and kept his eyes on the marble floor. "We are invisible," he told himself. But as the castle filled with soldiers, a curious thing happened to the unseen inhabitants. They found themselves swimming around the soldiers and up to the painted ceiling as though they were carried on water. And they saw the bright carpets and golden furniture floating slowly in a wide circle. It seemed that the whole building was turning like a great glass wheel.

The horsemen reached the edge of the cliff. They looked down at the wide, rushing river and turned their horses away. They moved back, never touching the circling furniture and the swimming children and then, suddenly, one of the soldiers stopped.

"What's that?" The man poked his finger through the clear glass wall. He touched a carpet — the carpet trembled and sank to the ground. Furniture tumbled on top of it, and all the children felt the stab of a gloved finger in their ribs. But none of them made a sound.

Eri stood up. Timoken could see doubt in the wizard's face. The spell was incomplete. Somewhere there was a flaw.

"What is it, Hugh?" the commander called to the soldier whose finger now rested in the air.

"I felt something," said the man. "A piece of wool or cloth. And I saw colors."

Several of the others laughed, and one of them said, "Like you saw a pile of stones where there are none?"

But the man kept his finger where it was. He leaned forward and squinted into the room. "I can see something else," he said. "I can see . . . I can see . . ."

The wizard strode toward the man. Timoken felt his heart slide into his mouth. Eri and the man were now staring at each other. All at once, the wizard lifted his staff and tapped the man's finger with its point.

The soldier grimaced. "Ow!" He ripped off his glove and sucked his finger. "Something bit me!"

This was followed by a howl of laughter from the men nearest to him. Even the commander gave a wide grin. "Come on, Hugh," he said. "It's the drink that's bitten you."

The man pulled on his glove. Still frowning, he followed his commander out of the castle and into the trees.

The children looked at one another and began to giggle, softly at first, and then, as the soldiers moved away, they rocked with unrestrained and happy laughter.

As soon as they were on their feet again, the walls became solid, the carpets were all in place, and the furniture looked as if it had never moved.

"It's ours, all ours," Sila declared, clapping her hands, "and no one will ever find us, no one will take our castle away from us, will they, Eri?"

The wizard yawned. "Not if I can help it." He lowered himself onto the couch.

"That soldier saw something," Thorkil remarked. "There's a flaw somewhere in the wall of plants."

"A small gap," the wizard said airily. "Easily repaired. Horses can kick things about a bit. But the spell is still there, nothing can move it now."

That evening, Timoken lit the candles in the long hall, identical to the one where his parents had dined with their friends and ministers. The cooking pots were put to use and a feast of sorts was laid out on the wide table: a feast of celebration. They had scarcely begun when Enid flew into the courtyard beyond the hall. With beating wings and excited squawks, she called, "People in the forest."

Timoken left the table and ran into the courtyard. "More people? Where?" he asked.

"By the river," said Enid. "They have horses."

Timoken looked into the candlelit hall. Reluctant to disturb the others, he lifted into the air. Only Gabar saw him flying into the dark sky; the camel was glad to see the dragon follow his family out into the night

Far below, a lamp swung in the breeze from the river, its light reflected in small wavelets that brushed the bank. Timoken could just make out three horses with, maybe, five riders. They were not soldiers, and yet he was wary of calling out. And then he heard a voice.

"Look! Up there! Is it a bird — or Timoken?"

"Mabon!" cried Timoken.

He swooped down, landing beside Mabon's horse. "Mabon, you're alive. You didn't die. I didn't kill you!" cried Timoken.

"You almost did!" Mabon slipped off his horse and gave Timoken one of his great bear hugs. "But your cloak gave me life again."

There was a touch on Timoken's arm, and there was his sister, with the biggest smile he had ever seen on her beautiful face.

"Zobayda," he cried, clasping his sister. "We have our home back, just like Mother said we would. We're safe."

Zobayda was too happy to speak, and then Edern was grabbing his hands and Peredur was throwing an arm around his shoulders.

"I thought I would never see you again," said Timoken, the tears in his eyes blurring their wide smiles. "But here we all are, the eagle, the wolf, and the bear. . . ."

"Sadly, not the fish," said Edern. "But we'll get Gereint back one day."

"And the running hare?" Timoken peered into the darkness. He saw a boy sitting on Mabon's horse. He wore sealskin breeches and looked familiar to Timoken. But he was not Beri. "Is she here?"

His friends were silent. Their smiles vanished and they looked at one another with grave faces. Zobayda said gently, "We lost her, Timoken. She escaped with us but those brutes Aelfric and Stenulf attacked us and we scattered. I looked for her everywhere."

"Your sister wouldn't give up," said Edern. "She searched half the night, but they must have caught our running hare."

Timoken couldn't speak. In the midst of such overwhelming happiness he couldn't understand why a dark cloud had descended, why his heart had stopped beating, and the castle behind him didn't seem quite so splendid after all.

CHAPTER 19
The Wizard's Grandchild

Seven days had passed since the escape. In that time, autumn had turned to winter. Wind and rain had stripped the trees of their last leaves. Now it was snowing.

Beri had found a cave where animals had lived. A lynx and her young, perhaps? It didn't smell too good, but it was warm and dry; the lynx had left a pile of fur on the floor and a few bones. The baby liked to play with them, and yet he wasn't playing, Beri decided. He was intensely involved with the bones, murmuring to himself and stroking their hard, bleached surfaces.

He was an extraordinary baby. He often demanded to be allowed to walk and, in spite of the thick undergrowth, could travel quite a distance on his short, sturdy legs. He never cried and could eat almost anything with his few baby teeth. He had never talked in the castle, but here, in the forest, he learned two or three new words every day.

The temperature plummeted and frost laid a sparkling crust on the snow. Zobayda had dressed the baby in warm clothes: a fur bonnet and a long coat made of sheep's wool. On his feet, he wore soft leather boots. Beri was also dressed for winter. She wore a thick padded jacket and woolen breeches. Zobayda had given her a hareskin cap with two fur streamers hanging down the back, and a pair of leather mittens. The enchanted sword in its leather scabbard was now buckled to Beri's belt.

The horse was sleeping on his feet, just inside the entrance to the cave, where at least it was dry. After two days, the snow stopped. It was time to move on.

"You'll have to ride now," Beri told the baby, "or you'll drown in snow."

He laughed. "Snow," he said. "Drown." He insisted on bringing one of the bones with him. It was a long thighbone but Beri didn't know what creature it came from. It could have been human.

Where were they going? To find Timoken, that's all Beri

knew. Someone had said north, and so that was the route she took. She wondered if Zobayda and the boys had escaped. Her terrified horse must have carried her in the opposite direction from the others. By now they were probably miles away.

She was aware that the horse was leaving a trail of prints in the snow, but there was nothing she could do about it. She could only hope that the search had been called off. "Let that bewhiskered brute find another wife," she muttered.

"Wife," said the baby, and they both laughed.

They had traveled less than a mile when the baby turned and looked up into her face, saying, "Go!" Anger and fear glimmered in his dark gray eyes.

Beri kicked the horse and he tried to gallop. Leaping over a fallen branch, he stumbled when he landed and Beri slipped off the saddle. She fell into a tangle of snow-covered creepers with the baby on top of her. The horse got to his feet snorting nervously, and then he bolted into the trees.

"Come back, you idiot!" cried Beri. "Come back!" She stood up with the baby clutching at her coat. "Silly horse," she told him. "If we don't catch him, it'll take us days and days to find the others."

"Walk," said the baby.

"Yes, walk." Beri was glad that she still had the bag of provisions strapped to her back. "Do you want to be carried?" she asked the baby.

"Walk!" he said with a determined frown.

And so they trudged onward, following the trail of deep prints left by the horse. The light was fading when Beri spotted him, grazing on a few stalks poking out of the snow.

"Stay here," she told the baby, "by this tree."

"Here!" he said.

As quietly as she could, Beri plodded through the snow toward the horse. Suddenly, she heard a sound to her left: a *thump*, a rustle of snow, and then another *thump*. Two figures bounded from behind a tree. Soldiers. They stood between Beri and the horse, their wide grins showing black and broken teeth.

"Well, if it isn't Sir Osbern's runaway wife," said Aelfric.

"I'm no one's wife." Beri spat the words.

"Will be soon," scoffed Stenulf.

"Never his!" Beri's hand flew to her sword hilt; drawing out the sword, she held it across her body.

"Ah. We want to play at fighting, do we?" Aelfric snorted with laughter at Beri. He sounded like a pig.

"If you want to play, you've chosen the wrong person." Beri sprang forward, her sword pointed at Aelfric's throat.

With a derisive sneer, Aelfric stepped toward her through the snow. Withdrawing his sword, he brandished it before her. Quick as lightning Beri beat his sword away with her own. He looked surprised, but as she lunged at him again, he brought his heavy weapon crashing down on hers.

"Come home, there's a good girl," called Stenulf.

Ignoring him, Beri danced around Aelfric, thrusting at his back, his arms, his chest.

Amazed by her skill and agility, he nevertheless managed to parry all her blows. He scratched her shoulder and her wrist, but she was too quick for him to do any damage.

"If that's what you want," he snarled breathlessly, "we'll have to take you back dead!" He turned and lifted his sword, ready to bring it crashing down on Beri's skull.

The sudden, shrill cry took them both by surprise.

The soldiers hadn't seen the baby. They stared at him, so tiny, the snow almost up to his waist.

"Drown!" His baby-cry rang through the trees. He lifted the thighbone and flung it at the sky. The two soldiers watched the bone in fascination as it twisted in the air above them. A grimace of disbelief crossed Stenulf's face when the bone became a knife, its lethal tip glinting in the snow light. Before he had time to gather his wits, the blade had entered his eye.

Beri thought his terrible scream would never end. Before it did, she leaped as her father had taught her; she leaped for her life, with her sword held straight and steady, and she lunged. Aelfric gave a mighty roar and struck at Beri's arm. But he was too late. The tip of her sword pierced the chain mail just above his collarbone and sank into his throat. He dropped into the snow with hardly a sound.

"We must run," cried Beri, sheathing her bloody sword.

"Run!" said the baby as she swung him up into her arms.

Aelfric and Stenulf had not been alone. Others had followed them. She could hear them shouting behind her. Stenulf must have reached them before he collapsed.

The horse was nowhere to be seen.

Beri dared not think what might happen if the soldiers caught her now. She zigzagged through the trees, hoping to confuse her pursuers, but she knew she couldn't run forever. Already, she had an ache in her side, her legs wouldn't run anymore, and the cold air in her lungs made her dizzy.

"I'm sorry," she whispered to the baby. "I can't go on." She stopped, and letting him slide onto the snow, pressed her hand into her aching ribs.

The baby looked up at her and smiled. "Look!" he said, and he pointed at a gap in the trees. There was something there: a creature. Beri could see a crested head; a long, scaly neck; and wide wings covered in snow. For all its alarming appearance, the creature's golden eye looked kindly at her.

Before she could stop him, the baby was bounding through the snow toward the creature. It turned its head to greet him, and when the baby stroked the wide, flat snout, Beri was horrified to see thin puffs of smoke curling from its nostrils. The baby laughed delightedly and tried to scramble onto the creature's neck.

"No!" cried Beri, but the creature had already lowered its head and the baby crawled onto the small spines that ran down the back of its neck and into the snow that covered its body.

"Safe!" The baby held his hand out to Beri.

She shook her head.

"Good!" said the baby, patting the crested head.

The voices behind Beri grew louder. She could hear boots tramping through the snow. "Here! This way. See! She's losing blood!"

"Run!" shouted the baby, his small brow creased with worry.

And so Beri ran. She leaped onto the scaly neck behind the baby, and the great wings were raised on either side of her. Drifts of snow flew all about them as they lifted into the air, and when Beri looked down, she could see the group of soldiers staring up at them in silent astonishment.

The palace in the secret kingdom had been built for eternal summer. A balcony supported by pillars ran around the upper level of the courtyard. Beneath the balcony one could sit in a shady passageway, out of the heat of the fierce African sun. Now that it had become a British castle, changes had to be made.

In Britain, when snow fell, the north wind blew it into the passageway, where it piled into frozen drifts. Gabar was indignant. "You promised sand," he complained to Timoken, "not this icy rubbish." Gabar kept his other problem to himself. Occasionally, he had to share his quarters with three leopards, but he knew it would be useless to mention this.

The camel wasn't the only one to complain about the snow. Sometimes it blew from the courtyard into the dining hall and the room that had now been named the chamber of pictures. Eri suggested a barrier; it could be made with multiplied lengths of wood, placed between the pillars. The barrier would stop icy drafts and snow from blowing into their living quarters.

"Excellent," said Thorkil, and he led a group of volunteers out into the forest. They returned with seven long branches, and Timoken set to work.

Since Tumi's arrival, Sila and he had seldom been apart. Together with Karli, they swept the snow out of the passageway and then helped the others to carry the wood multiplied by Timoken into the spaces between the pillars.

Eri paced the snowy courtyard. The dragon had been gone for too long. Every day she patrolled the sky above the forest, watching for strangers. But winter held the country in an icy grip, and even the most intrepid hunters had been deterred from braving the forest's hidden dangers.

Eri looked into the sky. He shook his head and, brushing the snow from a stone seat, sat down and began to mutter to himself.

"The wizard's worried," said Tumi.

"It's the dragon," Sila told him, and then she added quietly, "I'm glad you're here, Tumi."

"Me, too," said Tumi.

Timoken looked at Eri. It was getting dark, but he knew that the wizard wouldn't move until Enid came back. Smiling to himself, Timoken picked up the knife he'd been using and began to etch a figure into the red stones of the wall. He had already covered three stones with words and pictures.

"I can see you and your camel," said Tumi, peering at the wall. "And there's Karli and Sila."

"And you, Tumi," said Sila, "in your sealskin breeches."

"I can see Eri and his dragon, and the three leopards." Karli leaned closer. "Why are you drawing us, Timoken?"

Timoken turned from the wall. "So that my descendant can find me."

"Your descendant?" Sila frowned. "What's that?"

"Hmm." Timoken searched for words. "My descendant is someone who comes after me, one of my children's children's children's . . . Well, someone with my blood who will be born maybe nine hundred years from now."

They stared at him, bewildered. How could a person who hadn't yet been born travel back through so many hundreds of years? But then a boy who had one foot in the realm of enchantments probably had a purpose that none of them would fully understand.

Sila was worried for Timoken. There had been a sort of sadness about him lately, as though, in building his castle and making it safe, something had been lost. "You don't have any children, Timoken," she pointed out.

"No," he agreed. "Not yet."

There was a sudden joyful shout from the courtyard. "She's here!" cried Eri.

The dragon dropped gracefully through the air and Eri stood back as her great wings swept the snow. There was someone on her back. No, two people. A boy with a hareskin cap and a baby.

The boy slid off Enid's back with the baby in his arms. Timoken stared at the boy, stared at the hareskin cap with its long streamers of fur, and then he was running. Leaping over the piles of wood, he raced across the courtyard.

"Running Hare!" cried Timoken.

The other children crowded into the passageway and watched in surprise as Eri took the baby, and Timoken hugged and hugged the boy covered in snow.

"I think that boy's a girl," said Sila.

"Of course it is!" said Edern. "It's Running Hare!"

For a moment, no one noticed Eri. He was holding the baby at arm's length, gazing into his smiling face. "My child," he murmured. "My child's child." And tears streamed down his cheeks.

Timoken saw the wizard's face. "What's wrong with Eri?" he said.

The others turned to look at the wizard.

"My child's child." Smiling through his tears, Eri held up the baby. "My grandchild."

"I knew he had wizard's blood," said Beri.

The rebels' children knew nothing of Beri's past, or the wizard's tragic history, but something joyful in the winter air made everybody cheer.

Interview with Jenny Nimmo

What inspired you to tell the story of Timoken, the Red King?

Once I had made up my mind that Charlie Bone's ancestor would be an African king, I found myself referring to this ancient king in every book in the series. But I could never decide why the Red King came to Britain. I found myself wondering more and more about this mysterious and elusive character, until I finally realized that in order to make the Children of the Red King series more satisfying and complete, I would have to write the Red King's story.

Despite your story taking place in different parts of the United Kingdom, Timoken is an African prince. Is there a particular reason you chose for Timoken to be of African descent?

I've always been interested in the features and characteristics we inherit from our ancestors. In the Magician Trilogy, my hero, Gwyn, inherits his gifts from an ancient Welsh magician. Gwyn has few friends and lives in an isolated farmhouse in the Welsh mountains. I wanted Charlie Bone to be connected to a much wider world than lonely Gwyn, so I gave Charlie an African ancestor. After all, Africa is where mankind began — so we are told.

Magic is a key element in many of your books, including Chronicles of the Red King and the Charlie Bone series, Children of the Red King. Why is that? And were you drawn to magical stories when you were a young reader?

When I was a child, I didn't want to read about children like me; I wanted to read about princes and princesses, goose-girls, shepherd boys, and talking animals. For a precious half hour or so, I could identify with the principal character in a fantastic world, where, with the aid of magic, they would inevitably overcome all the seemingly insurmountable problems stacked against them. When I began to write, I naturally wanted to use the genre that had so comforted me as a child.

Chronicles of the Red King tells the story of Charlie Bone's magical ancestor, the Red King. Yet you wrote the Charlie Bone books first. Was it hard to go back and imagine this powerful king as a child born without his full strength and magic?

At first I thought that it would be easy to write about the Red King as a boy, and then I realized that I knew very little about Africa or Spain in the twelfth century. So I did a lot of research, which might not be apparent in the books, but gave me the confidence to concentrate on my characters without being held up by worries about their environment. And I really enjoyed working on Timoken's gradual discovery and understanding of his new powers.

The bond between Gabar and Timoken is one of the most powerful relationships in the story. Is there a reason you chose for Timoken's closest companion to be nonhuman?

Gabar had no place in my early notes for *The Secret Kingdom*. He appeared quite without warning, but once he had arrived, I realized how necessary his friendship with Timoken would be. I knew, from the beginning, that Zobayda would disappear, and Timoken would long for human company. But his utter loneliness needed to be mitigated and a talking nonhuman seemed to be the perfect companion. I began to enjoy their strange and funny friendship so much that Gabar sort of "took me over."

Sun Cat, Flame Chin, and Star are magical leopards that protect Timoken. However, in your other series, they appear as house cats named Aries, Sagittarius, and Leo that protect Charlie. Why did their names and form change over the centuries? Without Timoken, have they lost some of their magic?

In the prologue to Children of the Red King #5, *The Hidden King*, the Red King changes his leopards into cats. He does this to hide them from hunters who would enjoy killing leopards. As cubs, the leopards were wrapped in the web of the last moon spider. This made them immortal and, although they don't have the physical strength of leopards, they still have the magic that the web gave them. Over the years Timoken's names for them are forgotten, and from one of his many descendants they acquire the names of astrological signs.

Do you have a favorite character in the Children of the Red King series? If so, who and why?

Uncle Paton is my favorite character in the Charlie Bone books. He reminds me of my guardian, who was very tall and quiet and mysterious. He would arrive at my boarding school quite unexpectedly, but always with a book for me. I loved him very much.

If you could have any one of Timoken's or his descendants' powers, which would it be and why?

If I could have any power I wanted, I would choose to fly. It would be so good to escape from noisy crowds, traffic queues, and bad situations, and then have a bird's-eye view of the world below.

In what ways, if any, do your theater and television background affect the stories you imagine?

When I was about nine or ten, I was enchanted by the thought that actors could step into another world and, for a while, become someone different. Working in the theater was everything I had hoped for, and when I began to write, the excitement of entering another world was still with me, only now I could create that other world; and although I couldn't actually become another person in the same way as an actor, I could certainly leave my own character behind and identify with someone utterly unlike myself, a character whom I had created.

What books have inspired you the most?

Grimms' fairy tales were my favorite stories when I was a child. They were the reason that I used fantasy when I began to write. In *The Mabinogion*—a collection of Welsh legends—I found my first real hero, Gwydion the magician. It was his story that inspired the Magician Trilogy, and now, under another name, he plays a part in the Chronicles of the Red King. Authors need a language to convey their ideas, and Bruce Chatwin's work, especially his novel *On the Black Hill*, has had the greatest influence on my writing.

Where is your favorite place to write?

My favorite place to work in is a small room in my home with a window overlooking the river. It used to be my daughter's bedroom, and the blue sky and white clouds that she painted on her wall are still there, so that sometimes, I feel as though I'm flying.

What advice would you give to aspiring writers?

To an aspiring writer I would say: Read as much as you can and use the genre that you most enjoy. Create strong characters that you — and therefore your reader — can totally empathize with. Read your work aloud — it's surprising how many mistakes will come to light. If it sounds good, it will be good to read. Have patience. Keep writing, even if your work is not immediately accepted.

What are you working on now?

Right now I am writing about the Red King's ten children. I'm having a great time choosing the moments when each one of the children begins to discover their own peculiar endowment.

JENNY NIMMO

I was born in Windsor, Berkshire, England, and educated at boarding schools in Kent and Surrey from the age of six until I was sixteen, when I ran away from school to become a drama student/assistant stage manager with Theater South East. I graduated and acted in repertory theater in various towns and cities.

I left Britain to teach English to three Italian boys in Amalfi, Italy. On my return, I joined the BBC, first as a picture researcher, then assistant floor manager, studio manager (news), and finally director/adaptor with *Jackanory* (a BBC storytelling program for children). I left the BBC to marry Welsh artist David Wynn-Millward and went to live in Wales in my husband's family home. We live in a very old converted water mill, and the river is constantly threatening to break in, which it has done several times in the past, most dramatically on our youngest child's first birthday. During the summer, we run a residential school of art, and I have to move my office, put down tools (typewriter and pencils), and don an apron and cook! We have three grown-up children, Myfanwy, Ianto, and Gwenhwyfar.